HIS GIRL, HIS RULES

MORGANNA WILLIAMS

Published by Stormy Night Publications and Design, LLC.
www.StormyNightPublications.com

Cover design by Korey Mae Johnson
www.koreymaejohnson.com

Images by The Killion Group and Bigstock/PlusONE

1st Print Edition. February 2016

ISBN-13: 978-1530108558

ISBN-10: 1530108551

FOR AUDIENCES 18+ ONLY

This book is intended for adults only. Spanking and other sexual activities represented in this book are fantasies only, intended for adults.

PROLOGUE

Gabriel studied the sleeping form of his wife, doing his best to ignore the slow beep of the machine recording her heart rate and respiration. Both were slow; too slow.

He would lose her soon. Gabriel squeezed his eyes shut against the burning building behind them; how was he supposed to do this? He was her protector, it was his job to shield her from the rougher sides of life and keep her safe sometimes even from herself.

But he hadn't been able to protect her from this: cancer... the very name of his enemy filled him with rage. Rage he couldn't give voice to because she needed him to be calm and loving. They both knew they were at the end of their story.

The thought of saying goodbye to her, his sweet little submissive wife, brought such pain he had to fight to take a breath. It was like the very air in the room seared his lungs. He loved her so much and she was being taken from him.

"Gabriel?" Michelle's weak voice called to him as her small figure stirred in the bed.

Scrubbing a quick hand over his face, Gabriel made himself smile at her as he sat down in the chair next to her bed. "I'm here, baby girl."

She reached her small thin hand out to clasp his as he leaned in close. "Gabriel, I wanted to talk to you. I know you don't want to talk about this, but I need to say it."

He frowned as he studied the serious expression on her beautiful face. "What is it, love?"

"Gabriel, someday you will fall in love again…" she began.

"You're right, I don't want to have this conversation. I should paddle your little bottom for even bringing such a thing up. How could I ever want anyone else when I've had you?" he asked sternly.

Michelle smiled and lifted the hand not holding his to stroke the side of his face. "My darling man, you say the sweetest things."

Gabriel caught her hand in his own and pressed a gentle kiss to her palm. "Enough of such foolish talk."

A frown puckered between her brows. "It isn't foolish, darling. You're a young man and you will love again. You have to!"

"Michelle…"

"Gabriel, don't you see, it will be testament to how well we loved each other that you are able to love again. You have too much love inside you to let it die with me. Promise me, Gabriel. Promise!" As tears began to gather in her soft blue eyes, he gave in.

"I promise." He was barely able to speak past the growing lump in his throat.

Sighing, she relaxed back against her pillows. "Thank you. I wanted to talk more, but I'm so tired."

"Don't try to talk anymore, sweet girl. Rest, I'll be right here," he told her, stroking the hand in his own as her eyes drifted shut.

As he watched, her breath became more and more shallow, and then without even a small sound to demonstrate it was coming, she left him and was gone.

The alarm on the machine rang shrilly and the hospice nurse, waiting as unobtrusively as possible in a chair in the corner, rose and turned it off before leaving to give Gabriel his privacy.

Gabriel knelt at his wife's bedside with his head resting on their still joined hands and wept.

CHAPTER ONE

Glory Walters grinned as her best friend Nat opened her birthday present. It was a pretty glass bottle fashioned into a hummingbird feeder with a metal holder. When she saw it, Glory had known it would be perfect for Nat's backyard.

"I love it! Thanks, Glory!" Nat smiled at Glory before moving on to open the rest of her presents.

"So I hear you wrote a book," Jessica, Nat's younger sister and also one of her childhood friends, said from the chair beside her. She'd known Nat and Jess since she and Nat were seven and Jess was six. There had been more moments than she could count when she really wanted to gag Jess.

Glory blushed and looked nervously around to see if anyone had heard. "Shhh, I don't want to talk about this right now."

"Why? Is it a dirty book?" Jess asked with a raised brow.

If possible, Glory felt her face get even redder in response to the question. Point in fact it was BDSM erotica, but she was hardly going to say that out loud at a dinner party. There was a reason she shared the information with Nat but not with Jessica. It wasn't that she feared Jess' judgment; it was her complete lack of filter.

"Nat seems to be having a good time," Glory said in an effort to shift Jessica's attention.

"You didn't answer my question," Jess persisted.

Glory heaved a heartfelt sigh, and whispered out of the side of her mouth, "Yes, it's a dirty book, now hush."

"Morning Glory Walters!" Jess exclaimed loudly.

Glory winced and crossed her eyes as she did every time someone said her full name out loud. She loved her mother, but was that the best flower name she could think of? Hyacinth would have been better!

"Shhhhh," Glory said urgently as people began to look over at them. If her face got any hotter, she would burst into flames.

"I don't understand. Don't you have to be dirty before you can write about being dirty?" Jess asked.

Glory shrugged, trying hard to pretend the conversation wasn't happening and taking a drink of her sweet tea.

"I mean, that would be like me writing about being Asian."

Glory promptly choked on her drink. Jessica helpfully pounded her on the back until her pipes cleared.

"Thanks." Glory bit the word out with a glare.

"It was funny, Glory, admit it!" Jess said with an unrepentant grin.

Glory sighed. It had been a funny comment and Jess was just being Jess. "Fine, it was somewhat amusing," she said grudgingly.

Jessica laughed. "You know you love me, Glory."

"Yes I do, but sometimes I still think about killing you in your sleep!" she said crossly.

"Ooh, I think about killing Jess in her sleep too!" Nat said, jumping in on the conversation with a grin as she plopped down in the chair next to Glory.

"So what will be your focus this next year?" Glory asked her friend. Every year on their birthdays, they each picked something new to work on or accomplish.

"This year I am going to get that partnership in my

firm," Nat said with determination. "It's time; I either get the partnership they've been dangling for years or I'll start my own law practice."

Jessica and Glory both cheered loudly in response to Nat's words. It was past time the partners in her law firm recognized all of her hard work and all the cases Nat had won for them.

Nat turned her attention back to Glory. "Your birthday is next month; what are you going to do next year?"

Before Glory could say anything, Jessica chimed in, "I think Glory should make finally losing her virginity her goal this year."

"Jess!" Glory and Nat both hissed at the loudly spoken words and looked around to see if anyone had heard her outburst.

Jessica snorted, "Come on, Glo, you're about to be thirty-five. It's time to give it up. You must be the oldest living virgin in history. I mean, seriously, are there cobwebs up there?"

Glory felt her face flame anew, which had always been a constant state around Jess. "Geez, Jess, it's not like it doesn't get any action."

"Battery-operated boyfriends so do not count!" Jess declared.

Nat looked thoughtfully at Glory. "You know, she has a point. Think of it as research for your next book."

Glory felt all flustered as the focus of both of her friends shifted to her sex life. Were they really talking about this in a crowded restaurant?

"I need a drink," Glory said.

"I second that!" Jess said and then called a server over to order a round of tequila shots.

By the third round Glory was warming to the idea; by the fifth she'd convinced herself it had been her own. "It's perfect. My next story is set in a BDSM club, something frankly I have always had a little more than idle curiosity about. Perhaps in that setting I could finally relax enough to let go. It'll be great!"

"Um, Glory, I was thinking more along the lines of you sleeping with a guy you were dating. I'm not sure jumping into the deep end without your swimmies is the best idea," Jess said.

Nat chewed her lower lip worriedly. "Glo, this doesn't sound like a great plan to me. What if you end up with some hard-case dom who really hurts you?"

"That's why they have safewords," Glory said with a sloppy grin. She was really warming to the idea; the thought was bringing delightful tingling warmth to rest at the juncture of her thighs. She would definitely break out her B.O.B. as soon as she got home.

CHAPTER TWO

Studying her reflection critically in the mirror, Glory tried to decide if she could summon up the necessary confidence to walk into a BDSM club garbed in the short black skirt and purple bustier.

Glory was happier with her body than she had been in a long time; she'd worked hard to lose weight, but maybe she needed to lose more before trying to implement her plans.

"You look fabulous, Glory!" Nat said from behind her, meeting Glory's eyes in the mirror.

"I don't know..." She chewed her lower lip as she studied her overblown curves. "Maybe I should wait until I lose more weight."

"You look wonderful! There isn't anything wrong with being a size sixteen! I wish I had a fraction of your curves," her friend told her earnestly.

Glory rolled her eyes, Nat was perfect. Tall and slim with long blond hair and big blue eyes, she never had any shortage of dates; men flocked around her in droves. "Don't be silly, Nat, you're perfect, and why would you want to look like this?"

"I've always wanted boobs and hips. I might as well be a boy! Don't get me wrong, I do fine with what God gave me, but you look like a goddess."

"Don't get carried away, Nat, your nose is growing and in a minute you'll be so full of it your eyes will turn brown." Glory sighed and tried to look at herself with a little more objectivity. The bustier pulled her waist in tight, accenting her hourglass shape. Granted, it was a lush hourglass, but the shape was there just the same.

"You look like the silhouette some truckers have on their mud flaps," Nat said with a grin. "Men will line up, trust me."

Glory shook her head. "I might not have been a size sixteen since I graduated from high school, but I do remember there were no lines."

"We aren't talking about little boys here, Glory, we're talking about men with a capital M, totally different kettle of fish," her friend assured her. "You can't back out now, you have to do this, and you owe it to yourself. This is your year, remember?"

With one last look at the mirror, Glory straightened her shoulders determinedly. "Yes, it's my year. I'm tired of just writing about sex; it's time I experienced it for myself."

"I've been waiting on you to take action for years. No offense, hon, but you seriously do have to be one of the oldest virgins in history. Add the fact that you write erotic romance into the mix and the irony is almost enough to slay me."

Glory blushed. She loved Nat and couldn't ask for a better friend, but being a thirty-five-year-old virgin wasn't something she liked to talk about out loud with anyone. On her birthday after consuming a whole bottle of wine by herself, she'd mapped out the plan previously discussed at Nat's birthday party.

She was really going to take the bull by the horns, determined another birthday wouldn't pass without her experiencing some of the things she wrote about.

For years Glory had waited for love, sure that if she was patient, her Prince Charming would show up and sweep her off her feet. But princes seemed to be in short supply and love was even more elusive. Nope, she was done waiting for love. At thirty-five, she was an independent woman and probably way too set in her ways at this point to be able to live with another person.

Glory didn't need love, but hot sex was another story. It was her year and she was going to get her some. She'd found a local BDSM club doing research for an earlier romance novel. Spanking, bondage, and light D/s play had figured into her fantasies since before she knew what to call her kink or how widespread it was.

She'd made friends with one of the co-owners of the club when interviewing her extensively for the previous novel. Simone was only too happy to help her get her feet wet in the BDSM scene.

Tonight was the club's monthly munch to vet new members. Glory planned to be there and hopefully find someone to fulfill her fantasies. It would provide great information for the novel she was currently working on and scratch an itch that had needed taking care of for years.

Nat had helped her to find the bustier and short black skirt, and then done her hair and makeup. She'd piled Glory's long auburn curls on top of her head in an artful design of deceptive disarray, and subtle makeup accented Glory's slightly tilted hazel eyes, bringing out the green.

Glory had to admit she'd never looked better. Nat had managed to make her eyes look big and a little mysterious; her high cheekbones stood out above her full lips and stubborn chin.

Looking at the time, Glory took a deep breath and slid her feet into the four-inch heels that completed her outfit. It was now or never.

"I'm worried about those heels, Glory. You should really rethink them," Nat said, looking at her friend's feet with a frown.

"I can't wear flats! Not to this club; heels are what all the women wear!" Glory exclaimed.

"But you're a klutz," Nat pointed out rather bluntly. "You can't walk across a floor barefoot without falling over something non-existent."

"I'll be careful," Glory said, setting her chin stubbornly. If she was going to do this, she was going to do it right. It would be bad enough for her to be the only virgin in the room; she wasn't going to be wearing dowdy shoes too!

• • • • • • •

Glory sat nervously at a side table in the club lounge area, filling out a very detailed questionnaire about her limits. How was she really supposed to know what her limits were?

Obviously oral and vaginal sex were okay; anal sounded really interesting and had played a large part in her fantasy life for years, though she'd never had enough courage to put her B.O.B. into action there.

She chewed the top of the pencil eraser as she studied the different acts on the form: water sports… nope; bondage… that one was okay; verbal and physical humiliation… Glory pictured someone calling her names or pointing out her many flaws… big no to that. Just the thought of it was enough to bring tears to her eyes; nope, she'd had more than enough of that in high school and sadly in everyday life as well. People could be so mean!

Glory wasn't sure she even understood everything on the questionnaire, so she did the best she could filling it out and just said no to anything she didn't fully understand.

Simone set her up to meet with one of the partners in the club, Master Gabriel, after the munch and told her he would explain anything she didn't understand and give her a little experience with light play.

Glory was relieved Simone had been so open to her doing research for her book and exploring personally for herself. Simone told her as long as she didn't write specifically about club members, and everyone she interviewed was told why she was interviewing them, there shouldn't be any problems.

She looked around the room at the different people attending the munch and wondered which one was Master Gabriel. Simone had told her he would be the perfect master to introduce her to the club.

CHAPTER THREE

Gabriel grinned as he watched the redhead fill out the form, periodically flushing deeply as she read something, then squirming in her seat before taking a deep breath to answer the question. She also had the endearing habit of chewing on the end of her pencil as she concentrated on what she was reading.

He'd been watching her since he came down from the apartment he lived in above the club.

"That's the author," Simone said, as she watched him watch the redhead.

Gabriel frowned incredulously as he looked at Simone. "The little redhead blushing like a house on fire is the erotica author I'm meeting with later?"

Simone laughed. "Yep. Glory Walters aka Eva Grey. She is quite unexpected, isn't she?" The domme eyed the writer with a speculative gleam in her eye.

"Delicious," Gabriel said softly. He didn't know what Ms. Walters' story was yet, but he wanted to, and he also already knew he didn't want to share. He was intrigued over the disparity between her writing and how easily she seemed to embarrass. Gabriel hadn't experienced this level of interest since he lost Michelle. It was a mystery he'd have

13

the answer to before she left tonight.

It had been a long time since he'd felt such a need to possess a woman. He'd felt a fleeting lust for some since his wife died four years ago, but not this level of need.

Simone grinned and patted his arm. "I knew Glory would be the one to wake the sleeping dom. I've missed you, Master Gabe."

"What are you talking about? I've been here and I've been playing almost every weekend." He frowned at the woman next to him.

"You've been going through the motions, but you haven't really engaged; I see a light in your eyes I haven't seen since... well, I haven't seen it for a long time."

Gabriel's look softened. "I just needed some time to heal."

"Michelle was a wonderful woman, we all miss her, but she would have wanted you to be happy again."

"I know. She'll always be in my heart, but I've been at a place to make room in there for someone else too for a while now. This is just the first time I've seen a woman who made me want more than a night," he told her honestly.

"Like I said, the sleeping dom has awoken," Simone said softly before walking away.

• • • • • • •

Glory fidgeted nervously on the couch in Master Gabriel's office, trying to make her short skirt cover more of her rounded thighs and trying to ignore the man watching her. He was absolutely beautiful with black hair that curled slightly around his ears, sparkling blue eyes set in a strong face with a squared jaw and topped with dimples. He was tall with broad shoulders and was obviously very fit; in a nutshell, she was way out of her league.

She felt her eyes widen in alarm when he sat down next to her a little closer than she was comfortable with. Good night Irene, but the man was hot! Sex on a stick as Jessica would say.

She swallowed as her mouth seemed to completely dry up and her pulse began to pound in her ears. Master Gabriel was like every fantasy man she'd ever dreamed up in one muscular package of alpha-ness.

Glory blinked in alarm when he suddenly snapped his fingers in front of her nose. "Ms. Walters? I've been talking to you. Where did you go off to?"

She felt hot color fill her cheeks as she looked over at him. "I'm sorry, Master Gabriel, I was woolgathering." Glory looked down, embarrassed that she was messing up this interview so badly.

Firm fingers caught her beneath the chin and brought her head up so she had no choice but to meet his steely gaze. "No more woolgathering, young lady. Now, I asked you why you were here."

"I, umm, needed to do some research for my new novel... and... I... well... umm..."

"I think it's safe to say since you filled out a membership questionnaire that you have a more personal interest in BDSM than research. Correct?" he asked, pinning her with his knowing eyes.

"Yes," she said softly, the penetrating eye contact making her feel like he could see straight into her soul.

"Yes, sir," he corrected her.

"What?" Glory blinked, freeing herself from his eyes for a moment.

"You will call me sir while we're in this room. Understood?" he asked with a brow raised questioningly.

"Yes, sir," Glory answered.

"Good girl. Now, are you ready to explore your submissive nature this evening?" Once again his blue eyes captured hers, allowing her no escape.

"Yes, sir," she said with a soft sigh. The normal protest dying on her lips, Glory found she couldn't deny this compelling man. She wanted to please him.

He smiled at her, his blue eyes suddenly warm as they

crinkled at the corners. "Then we will begin. Your safeword for tonight is red."

Then suddenly his hands were at her waist and he lifted her easily to sit on his lap facing away from him.

Glory gasped, her hands going instinctively to wrap around his wrists.

"Glory, let go of my hands, please," he said firmly.

She immediately let go. "I'm sorry, sir. I'm not used to being picked up."

"It's alright, sweetness, but I need your hands out of the way." His firm hands caught hold of her wrists and lifted them over her head to place them behind his neck. "I want you to hold onto the back of my neck right now. Don't move them until I tell you to. Understand?"

"Yes, sir." Glory tried not to think about the way the position lifted her breasts up and out. They looked ready to pop out of the top of the bustier.

"Good girl," he said soothingly and then he brought his hands up under her skirt and hooked his fingers in the waistband of her panties, slowly tugging them down. She lifted her hips slightly as he worked them off then pulled them down her legs.

Her breath came out in a deep shuddering gasp as she watched him tuck them into his pocket before catching her under each thigh and lifting her legs to straddle his. Cool air kissed her hot center when he spread his legs, opening her wide.

Big hands skimmed up her legs, catching the hem of the short skirt and tucking it into her waistband, then stroked slowly up her torso until they came to rest beneath her breasts. Gabriel kissed the side of her neck as he pulled the top of her bustier down until her breasts popped free and into his waiting hands.

"Beautiful," he murmured against her neck as he cupped a breast in each hand and began to rhythmically pluck her nipples between his thumbs and forefingers.

Glory groaned and arched her back even more, pressing

her breasts more tightly into his hands as she gripped the back of his neck.

"So responsive," he said as he began to pull and twist each nipple a little harder, causing the sweetest pain she'd ever felt.

"Ooohh!" Glory was awash in sensation. The feel of his hands on her breasts was almost too good and the scent of her arousal filled the air as the telltale slickness between her legs leaked to her inner thighs.

Needing more, she moved her legs restlessly on either side of his legs as he continued to play with her breasts.

"What do you want, little sub?" Gabriel asked, pulling hard at her nipples and wringing another groan from her lips.

"I need…"

"What do you need?" he asked insistently.

"Please… touch me," she whimpered.

"I am touching you, Glory," Gabriel said with another hard tug that bowed her back.

"Not there. I want you to touch me… on my clit," she finished on a breathless whimper.

• • • • • • •

Gabriel decided to take pity on his little sub and moved his hands from her breasts down her rounded tummy, one hand holding her down as the other cupped her hot, wet mound.

He slid his fingers into her dripping heat as the palm of his hand ground against her swollen little clit. "Is this for me?"

She tried to buck her hips up to press against his hand, but the firm palm on her belly prevented it. "Please…" she begged softly.

"Answer me, young lady. Is this for me?"

"Yes, sir!" Glory cried out as he rewarded her by thrusting one finger deep inside her tight sheath.

17

She was so tight, gripping his finger as he moved in and out gently, swirling it around inside her a few times before pulling out and thrusting back inside with two fingers.

Her hands gripped his neck harder and harder as he increased the speed of his fingers. Gabriel smiled, feeling her walls begin to flutter around him as she built toward orgasm.

"No!" she yelled in protest when he stilled the movement of his hand. "Please, sir. Please!"

"You don't get to come until I give you permission, Glory. Shhhhhh, it's okay, baby, you'll get there, I promise." He soothed her when she gave a soft mewling little cry of protest.

He moved his legs further apart, spreading her even wider as he began to scissor his fingers inside her, stretching her impossibly tight canal before pulling out and coming back to press three fingers in deep.

Gabriel moved his other hand down from her belly to spread her lips wide as he began to thrust his fingers in and out of her hard and fast.

She began to cry out softly in a long drawn-out moan as she rode his fingers, her hands clenching down so tightly on his neck he was sure he'd have some marks.

"Now, Glory," he told her firmly as he flicked her clit with the tip of one finger and she came with a shuddering cry, her body milking the fingers continuing to move in and out of her relentlessly.

"Again," Gabriel said as he caught her sweet little clit between his thumb and forefinger and pinched it hard. This time she screamed when she came, her back bowing so hard he had to catch her with one arm to keep her on his lap.

Then she relaxed in his arms, slumping against his chest, her head lolling back on his shoulder.

"Good girl. You did very well, Glory," he said, kissing her cheek as he lazily stroked his free hand up and down her side.

• • • • • • •

"That was amazing," Glory said as soon as she was able to catch her breath. "I never knew it could be like that. I thought I'd had orgasms before but that would be like comparing a piddly little wave with a tsunami," she said with a laugh, stretching luxuriously. "But maybe it's just different when someone else is giving you the orgasm."

Her B.O.B. had certainly never come close to nearly making her spontaneously combust. Master Gabriel, on the other hand, should have come with a warning label. She grinned as she pictured a placard hanging from his neck saying *Warning: dangerously explosive orgasm. Come at your own risk.*

The hand stroking her side so sweetly stilled. "You've never had an orgasm with a lover before?"

"I've never actually had a…" Glory froze as she realized what she'd almost revealed in her moment of afterglow. Sitting up straight on his lap, she pulled her arms from around his neck where she'd still had them, her fingers playing idly with the curls at the nape of his neck.

"Glory?"

She moved before he was able to realize her intent and jumped off his lap, pulling her skirt down to cover herself as well as she could and jerking the bustier up to cover her still pouting nipples. Glancing to where her panties poked out of his pocket, Glory decided they were a complete write-off. No way could she risk a retrieval mission; this man would know all her secrets in a heartbeat if he got his hands on her again.

Glory decided to attempt a blasé attitude about the whole situation, carefully avoiding eye contact by studying the floor. "Thank you for a great… well, it was great, but you know, I should really be going and I think…"

"Stop right there." Gabriel stalked over to where she stood fidgeting nervously in front of his desk and caught her under the chin with his fingers again. Forcing her to meet his penetrating stare, he asked, "What exactly have you never actually had, Glory?"

Caught once again in the steel trap of his eyes, Glory could only stammer. "I... ummm... well, I..."

A quick knock followed by the door opening saved her from answering. "Sorry to interrupt, Gabe, but we really need you out on the floor for a second," the domme, Simone, said from the doorway.

Gabriel straightened but didn't take his eyes off hers. "Glory, you will wait for me right here in this office. When I get back, I expect a real answer to my question. No more evasions, young lady."

Then she watched as he followed Simone from the office. Glory quickly gathered her purse and shoes and hurried from the room. No way was she going to stay and finish that conversation; she'd embarrassed herself enough for one evening, thank you very much.

It was too bad she couldn't risk exploring more of her sexual side with Gabriel; he was really good at it. Way too good for her to be able to hold her own without revealing more than she wanted to about herself.

It was time to go home.

• • • • • • •

Gabriel wasn't really surprised to return to the office and find his little sub had run away. He grinned. Little Miss Morning Glory Walters had a few things to learn about doms; one dom in particular.

She hadn't said her safeword and had left in the middle of a scene; as far as Gabriel was concerned the scene wasn't over. The venue had just changed.

Grabbing her membership application from his desk, he quickly entered her home address into his phone. On his way out the door, he patted the lacy black panties in his pocket. Simone was right; the sleeping dom had woken and he was about to claim his woman.

CHAPTER FOUR

Glory barely had time to change into her favorite flannel gown and wash her face before the doorbell rang.

She frowned; who would come over to her house this late? Maybe Nat and Jess couldn't wait until tomorrow to ask about her evening.

That had to be it! With a grin she swung the door open. "You couldn't wait until tomorrow?"

The sight of Gabriel standing on her doorstep with a pair of lacy panties in his hand brought her hand to her throat in alarm.

"I certainly couldn't, young lady," he said firmly, herding her back into her hallway and pushing the door closed behind him. "In the future you're not to answer the door without asking who it is and definitely not unless you're dressed."

Glory blinked up at him, still trying to process the fact that he was standing in her house at all, much less giving her instructions about stuff that wasn't really his business.

"Am I understood?"

"Huh?" she asked as she licked suddenly dry lips.

"I asked if I was understood," he explained helpfully.

"Understood about what? Why are you here?" Glory

21

asked. "We finished, didn't we?"

Gabriel quirked one eyebrow at her and folded his arms across his chest as he studied her, apparently prepared to wait her out.

She flushed and plucked at her gown anxiously. "I mean... we... well... I, er... I was kinda done and it was late... so..."

"Did I or did I not tell you to wait for me in my office?" he asked succinctly.

"Well... I... guess... sort of," Glory finished lamely, still avoiding eye contact.

"Morning Glory Walters, I asked you a question and I expect an answer," Gabriel said firmly.

She gulped, raising her flushed face to meet his stern gaze, "Oh, my gosh, did you just three-name me?"

"Glory." He said her name warningly.

"Okay. Yes! I confess! You told me to wait and I left. I was kind of in a hurry so I..."

"You panicked and ran away," Gabriel finished for her. "Our scene was not finished and you knew it."

"I must have misunderstood," she said rather lamely.

"Glory, you already have one punishment coming. Do you really want to add to it by lying to me?"

"P-punishment?" Glory began to back carefully down the hall away from the big dom. She felt very vulnerable standing there in just her nightgown without even a pair of panties underneath it.

Gabriel smiled and stalked slowly toward her, rolling up his sleeves as he advanced toward her retreating figure.

Glory's eyes widened at his approach, then she turned in a blind panic to run and ran straight into a wall. Gabriel caught her, politely preventing her fall when she bounced off the wall backwards straight into his arms.

• • • • • • •

Gabriel bit back a laugh at the startled expression in her

hazel eyes when she found herself back in his arms.

"Good girl," he told her with a grin as he steered her toward the living room with the arm he had wrapped around her waist. "It's always best to face a punishment immediately. I'm proud of you, sweetness."

"Wait... what? I wasn't... I mean, I..." Glory stammered as if she wasn't quite sure how she found herself standing between his legs as he sat down in the center of her cream-colored sofa.

"What do you have to say for yourself, young lady?" Gabriel asked her sternly, his eyes pinning her in place.

Her face filled with color. "I just couldn't stay and..."

"You didn't want to answer my questions." Once again he finished for her.

She looked down. "No, sir."

"Eyes on me, Glory," he barked. Her wide eyes sprang back up to his and her chin began to quiver quite enchantingly. "You knew I expected you to be waiting in my office when I got back."

"Yes, sir," she said softly, her shoulders rounding dejectedly.

"You were naughty, weren't you?" he asked her, watching her responses closely.

Eyes dilated, Glory gave a shudder before swallowing visibly and answering, "Yes, sir."

There it was: the delicious response of a submissive who knew she'd earned a punishment she both feared and craved.

"What happens to naughty little girls?" Gabriel asked her, continuing to hold her gaze.

She shuddered again, letting her breath out in a little gasp, before she squeaked her answer, "They get spanked."

"That's right, naughty little girls get spanked on their bare bottoms," he told her as he took her arm firmly and pulled her down over his lap.

"Wait! No! You can't!" Glory came back to life, struggling to roll off his lap, but Gabriel held her easily in place.

"Be still!" he said, delivering two crisp swats to her flannel-covered bottom.

"Oh!" she cried out as she jerked in response to the swift spanks.

"Why are you here?" Gabriel asked firmly. "Why are you over my lap about to get your bare bottom spanked?"

"Stop saying that out loud!" she yelled, beginning to twist her body a little frantically.

Again he held her easily in place, marveling at the deep red color filling her face and neck as she looked up at him over her shoulder in a panic. Shaking his head with a sigh, he pulled the hem of her gown up to reveal her naked backside.

"Obviously I need to help you focus on the issue at hand," he told her resolutely as he lifted his hand high and brought it back down hard on her white bottom. It bounced delightfully beneath his hand as he delivered swat after swat to her wriggling posterior.

"Oww! Ohh! Please! I'm sorry, sir!"

Raining his hand down hard and fast, Gabriel paid special attention to the under curve of her generous bottom as he delivered five swats to each sit spot. Then he stopped and stroked his hand over the area he'd just spanked.

"What are you sorry for, young lady?"

•••••••

Glory couldn't believe she was over a man's knee getting her bottom spanked. It hurt way more than it did in her fantasies. His hand was hard! His palm now rubbed over her stinging flesh and she felt a gush of wetness between her thighs.

"Glory?" His hand fell again in four sharp swats.

"Oww! I'm sorry I left. I should have waited for you in the office," she said in rush of breath. Did this mean her spanking would be over? Why did the thought of him

24

stopping make her want to cry?

"Very good, now that we've established the reason for your spanking, we can start your punishment," he told her soothingly as his hand continued to stroke her heated flesh.

Glory sighed, "Oh, good. Wait! What do you mean start my punishment?"

"Did you really think we were finished?" he asked in surprise.

"I didn't really know. It's not like this is an everyday occurrence or anything," she said with a hint of snarkiness. Did he think she'd read the spanking rulebook or something?

"That just increased the number of swats from twenty to forty, young lady," he told her sternly. "I'd keep the smart comments to myself if I were you."

"Yes, sir," she said softly.

She couldn't believe she was over a man's lap about to receive forty swats on her bare bottom for punishment. For years Glory had fantasized about a man taking her in hand quite literally, but now that it was happening she wasn't sure how she felt about it.

A loud clapping sound and a sudden stinging heat on her left cheek brought her out of her musings in a hurry. "Ouch!"

"Now that I have your attention again, are you ready to begin your punishment?" he asked as his large palm rubbed circles on her upturned backside.

"That one didn't count either?" she asked in alarm.

"I have quite a healthy self-esteem, but I really do expect a sub's attention on me and what I'm doing when spanking her. You will focus on your punishment without further side trips in your mind until I'm finished. Are we clear, young lady?"

"Yes, sir," Glory said with another heated blush filling her face.

Then his hand fell hard and fast and she found she couldn't do anything but focus on him, his hand, and the burning heat rapidly filling her poor vulnerable bottom.

"Ohh… oww… not so hard… not so fast… oohhhhh!" she cried and kicked, but he held her easily in place as his hand continued to fall in no discernible rhythm.

Tears were welling in her eyes and her bottom felt like it would burst into flame at any moment. Then he stopped and simply rested his hand on her heated flesh and Glory breathed a sigh of relief. It was over.

"Almost done, sweetness," he told her as he caught her chin to make her look over her shoulder at him.

Crap, it wasn't over!

"Remind me again why you're over my lap getting your naughty bottom spanked like a little girl?"

If her face got any redder, Glory was sure she'd spontaneously combust; between the blush and the intense heat in her seat, it seemed like a distinct possibility.

"You told me to wait for you in your office and I left," was her only answer.

"What should you have done?"

"Waited for you, sir," she said with a miserable little sniffle.

"Very good." He smiled at her then made a motion for her to put her face back down. "I plan to make these last ten memorable."

Then his hand slapped down hard on the crease between her thigh and bottom; she stiffened and yelped when it fell again just as hard in the exact same place. Her eyes widened in horror as she realized he was going to do five on each side.

"No! Not in the same place… please… ooooohh!" she cried as tears filled her eyes and spilled over to run down her cheeks.

Gabriel ignored her pleas and delivered exactly what he'd promised: ten swats, five to each sit spot, and part of her reveled in the fact that he hadn't given in to her pleas. Even though her bottom burned, she'd felt herself getting wetter and wetter throughout the punishment and the heat seemed to spread to other areas that wanted his attentions.

She groaned and arched her hips as the very palm that delivered her punishment began to stroke the hot, sore flesh of her bottom. When his fingers moved to press against the wet heat between her thighs, Glory moved her legs farther apart for him.

"Good girl. You're so wet and hot," Gabriel said as he sank two fingers deep inside her and began to move them in and out in an ever-increasing rhythm as he shifted her over his lap so her clit rode his knee with every inward thrust of his hand.

Glory's breath began to come in short panting gasps and every muscle in her body began to tighten in preparation for an explosive orgasm. Then his other hand shifted between their bodies so he could pluck and pinch at her clit as his fingers worked in and out of her mercilessly.

Her body coiled tighter and tighter as she got closer to the edge... just as she was about to explode, all movement stopped.

"Noooo! Please, sir... please..." she whimpered, desperate in her need for release.

"What were you going to say you'd never had earlier in my office, Glory?" Gabriel asked.

Glory couldn't think, she was so caught up in her need to come and the demanding pulse of her swollen clit between her thighs. "What?"

"When you said you'd never had an orgasm with a lover, you said you'd never actually, but then you didn't finish. I need you to finish that sentence, Glory. What have you never actually had?" he asked implacably.

The hands that had been about to send her into nirvana now held her still, preventing her from rubbing against him or pressing her legs together to relieve the ache of need.

Glory turned her head to look over her shoulder at him and glare, her lips tightening as she shook her head at him defiantly.

The grin she got in return should have warned her.

Gabriel worked three fingers back inside her and pressed his thumb into her back hole as he began to pluck again at her clit.

His broad thumb seemed to rotate inside her ass as he continued to relentlessly thrust those three fingers in and out of her pulsing sheath. All the while Gabriel's other hand continued to pluck and worry her poor abused clit until once again she was on the edge of shattering to pieces.

Again everything stopped, and Glory wailed in frustration.

"Answer the question, Glory," he said firmly.

"Bite me!" she snapped, then yelped as the fingers working her clit were removed so he could deliver three sharp swats to each side of her already sore bottom. Then the fingers returned to torture her throbbing clit anew while his fingers and thumb worked in tandem to drive her insane.

He worked her hard and fast, bringing her to the edge again and again, only to stop just before she could go over.

"Please... please... I need to come," she whimpered, tears of frustration and need falling from her as she begged.

"Answer my question, sweetness, and I'll let you come," he told her resolutely.

"Fine!" she shouted, glaring at him with tear-bright eyes. "I've never actually had a lover or had sex! I've never done the horizontal tango or mambo whatever you want to call it! I'm a virgin! Are you happy now?"

"Immeasurably," he told her with an unrepentant grin as he twisted his fingers high against some magical spot inside her and pinched her clit hard.

Glory came, screaming his name as she writhed in her position over his knee. She'd barely managed to catch her breath before he did it again.

When she came back to herself, she was sitting up straddling him, resting against his chest. She looked up at him; as soon as she met his eyes, he brought his fingers to his lips and licked them clean. She felt everything between her legs clench tight at the sight of him licking her essence off his fingers.

Then he cupped her face between his hands and leaned down to capture her lips. Glory had at least been kissed before, but nothing prepared her for the way he seemed to devour her.

His tongue sank deep, claiming every inch of her mouth for his own; his kiss reeked of possession. He demanded her surrender as he conquered her, and Glory gave him everything. It was as if he took her very breath and gave it back to her.

Then Gabriel pulled away after pressing one last soft kiss against her lips. "It's been a long night for you, sweetness. I think it's time for bed."

• • • • • • •

He smiled at the dazed confusion in her slumberous eyes; he pulled Glory to her feet and used a hand in the small of her back to guide her to her bedroom.

Gabriel almost laughed when he had to steer her away from the door frame of her bedroom just before she walked into it. How often did his little writer run into walls?

She stood nervously next to him as he turned down her bed then smiled down at her. "Climb into bed, sweetness. I'll tuck you in before I go."

"You're leaving?" she asked, her brow wrinkled as if she was trying to figure him out.

"Yes. It's only our second date. Way too soon for me to stay the night," Gabriel told her as he urged her under the covers and tucked them around her before treating himself to one last taste of her full lips.

"What? We're dating? When was our first date?" She fired the questions at him rapidly in a rush of breathlessness.

"Our first date was at the club. Our second date was your spanking, a tad unconventional I know, but necessary. Tomorrow night when I come to take you to dinner, it will be our third date and we can do a little more heavy petting without the spanking if you behave yourself," he told her with an admonishing tap to her nose.

"What about the club? I was going to be doing research as well as exploring my own curiosity at the club," Glory reminded him.

"I'm afraid the club is off limits for you for the near future," Gabriel told her firmly.

"What?" She sat up in bed with a frown. "Why? I need to go to the club. I didn't get to look around or interview anyone or…"

"Glory, you have no business in that club until you have a little more experience. You in the club is like someone learning to walk signing up for a marathon. So until further notice it's off limits for you," he explained.

"It isn't up to you!" Glory got up on her knees in the bed to yell at him. "I'm an adult and I can join a BDSM club if I want to. I don't need your permission."

"Morning Glory, you will settle down right now and listen. A virgin has no business in that club. It's dangerous enough for baby submissives, but you're new to sex in general," he told her.

"See, this is exactly why I had no intention of telling anyone I was a virgin! All it does is cause problems. I'll just go to a bar and pick up someone to take care of it or better yet hire an escort, and then it won't be a problem," she said, clearly dismissing him from her thoughts as she began to plot out her next course of action in her mind.

Gabriel took a deep breath to keep from expressing his outrage at the idea of another man touching what he already considered his; he reined it in and sat down next to her on the bed. Gently pushing her flat, he leaned down over her, gratified by the wary look in her wide eyes as she looked up at him.

"You will not be going to a bar and picking anyone up and you certainly won't be hiring an escort," he told her in no uncertain terms.

"I will do…" She blinked when he pressed a hand over

her mouth.

"Let me stop you before you land yourself back over my knee with less satisfactory results for yourself this time. You will do exactly as I say, young lady. You will date me and allow things to take their natural course. Glory, you deserve a little wooing and romance. We'll go back to the club when I feel you're ready and not a moment sooner."

"You're awfully bossy," she said after pushing his hand away from her mouth with a disgruntled look.

Gabriel grinned and pointed to himself. "Dom. Remember, sweetness?"

She smirked at him.

"My club. My girl. My rules," he said sternly.

"Your girl?" Glory asked with a raised brow.

"Yep. We'll go over the rest of your rules tomorrow after dinner. I don't have a lot, but you need to know going in that while I don't really consider myself a 24/7 dom, I will always be the alpha in this relationship and there will be rules you'll need to follow or face the consequences," he said matter-of-factly before leaning down to kiss her once more and tucking the covers back around her. "Go to sleep. I'll be here tomorrow at seven to pick you up for dinner."

She studied him for a minute, obviously thinking very seriously about everything he'd said; he saw the moment she'd come to a decision. Glory nodded to herself then looked up at him. "Yes, sir. I'll be ready."

"Good girl, now go to sleep. I'll let myself out." Gabriel leaned down and pressed a gentle kiss to her forehead before turning out the light and leaving the room.

Going from room to room, he made sure every door was locked up tight before leaving through the garage. He hit the button to shut the garage door and ran out underneath it before it closed.

No doubt about it, Glory was going to be a hard sell, but he had every intention of closing the deal.

CHAPTER FIVE

Glory woke feeling better than she had in years. Her body still tingling with remembered pleasure. She'd written about explosive multiple orgasms but had half believed it was all the stuff of fantasy and nothing she could ever expect in reality.

Thankfully in this instance she'd been wrong, because wow-oh-wow, was the reality hotter than anything she could have dreamed up. If the last orgasm Gabriel had given her had been any more intense, Glory was pretty sure she would have passed out.

And the spanking! A new surge of wetness pooled between her thighs as she thought about being across Gabriel's lap. It had hurt, but boy, had it ever tripped her trigger.

She wriggled around experimentally, shifting her bottom across the bed sheets, and frowned. Not a prickle of sting or any lingering soreness.

Frowning, Glory climbed from the bed and lifted her gown to study her backside in the full-length mirror next to her vanity.

Nothing! Her bottom was as white as it ever was; it was as if the spanking had never occurred. Why did that make her so sad?

She knew it wasn't the pain of the spanking that had aroused her as much as the complete mastery he'd demonstrated over her; the dominance of the act. The aftereffects, the heat and slight soreness in her bottom last night after he'd finished her punishment—that part she'd enjoyed. The actual punishment, not so much.

Though perversely she wondered what it would be like if he punished her for something more serious. She pictured him taking her back over his knee for something major and spanking her until she hung limply over his knee sobbing out her apologies. Would he make her stand in the corner with her hot red bottom on display?

Glory groaned out loud as the wetness and heat between her thighs grew exponentially. With a smile she opened the drawer of her bed stand and pulled out her trusty vibrator.

Lying back on the bed, she spread her legs wide, turning it on high as she thrust it straight inside her needy channel.

She wasn't in the mood to tease herself; her morning reverie had taken her way beyond the point of slowly building up her arousal. Glory wanted it hard and fast and she soon realized doing this on her back wasn't going to cut it.

Rolling over, she brought her knees beneath her and spread them wide; using one hand, she spread her lips open as she drove the vibe in hard and fast. Her hips began bucking down to meet it immediately, the little clit stimulator buzzing against her clit with every inward stroke. Finally needing more stimulation, Glory simply pressed it deep and ground it hard against her inner walls as the little vibrator rode her clit.

She pictured Gabriel's hard hand slamming down on her butt and then exploded around the sex toy with a muffled scream. Smiling, she began to move it in and out in a gentle rhythm as she rode out the final pulses of her orgasm, drawing it out as much as possible, and then collapsed face down on the bed to recover.

33

That had been the most intense orgasm she'd ever given herself; it still hadn't compared to the ones Gabriel had supplied, but it was still a pretty amazing solo venture.

Of course it hadn't really been solo; Gabriel had been there the whole time in her mind. Glory sighed; no way did she have any business falling for a man. Especially one like Gabriel.

Mr. Hot-sex-on-a-stick dom man.

Things were getting problematic.

• • • • • • •

Glory was ready at ten to seven despite her concerns about becoming a little too attached to Gabriel. When push came to shove, she wanted to experience everything he had to offer too much to deny herself the opportunity.

The doorbell rang before she had the chance to worry about it further and she opened the door to find Gabriel looking devastatingly attractive in a pair of well-worn jeans and a button-down shirt with the sleeves rolled up.

"You always answer the door without asking who it is?" he asked with a raised brow.

Glory barely managed to control her impulse to roll her eyes. "I knew it was you."

"It could have been anyone," Gabriel said succinctly.

"It wasn't, it was you," she pointed out matter-of-factly.

"Glory," he said sternly.

"Gabriel," she said back, raising her own brow. Glory recognized her mistake when his mouth tightened and he pushed his way inside past her. Uh oh, now the dom was coming out to play.

He caught her firmly by the arm and pulled her away from the door to swing it shut. then tucked her beneath one arm, pulled her over his hip, and hiked her skirt up to rest on her back.

"Gabriel! Stop! I…"

"You were testing me. When it comes to matters of

safety, young lady, I'm not playing, which you will fully understand before we leave this house."

Strong fingers hooked in the waistband of her panties as he tugged them down her hips and legs until they landed at her feet. "Step out and kick them to the side."

"What?"

A sharp swat landed on her exposed backside, making her yelp. "You heard me. Do it."

Glory swallowed at the implacable tone in his deep voice and immediately complied.

"Good girl. From now on, what are you going to do when someone knocks or rings your bell, young lady?" he asked, still holding her bent at the waist over his hip.

"Ask who it is?" she asked hesitantly.

"Exactly, just to make sure you remember…" Gabriel delivered a fast barrage of swats to her bottom, causing her to dance awkwardly in place while precariously balanced on four-inch heels.

When she was sniffling and about to give in to the tears rapidly filling her eyes from the growing discomfort in her bottom, he stood her back up in front of him.

He smiled and cupped her cheeks in his hands, framing her face and gently wiping the tears from under her eyes with his thumbs. "Do you think you'll remember to ask who it is in the future?"

"Yes, sir," Glory said, sounding like a lost little girl to her own ears.

"Good. Now go wipe your face and change your shoes, then we can go," Gabriel said as he turned her toward her room.

"Change my shoes? Why?" Her brow wrinkled in consternation.

"No offense, sweetness, but I've noticed you're a tad clumsy. I've seen you walk into walls, and I think those heels are courting a broken ankle."

Her back straightened in outrage. "I'm not that bad!"

He merely raised a brow at her again.

"Well, I admit I'm a little clumsy, but I can wear heels," she told him.

"Not anymore. One of the rules we'll be discussing over dinner is no heels. I don't want to risk you getting hurt."

"You can't just come in here and give me some arbitrary list of rules!" she snapped.

"I not only can, I am and while you're with me, young lady, you will follow them. I believe wholeheartedly in domestic discipline. I don't feel I'm being unreasonable, since all of the rules I expect you to follow have to do with safety, health, and your general well-being," Gabriel said sternly.

"You're completely impossible!" she charged before stomping from the room to do as he'd instructed. Why was she giving in to his demands? She was a grown woman! Glory couldn't believe she was letting him dictate footwear. Although she had almost changed a few minutes before he got there when she twisted her ankle falling off the shoes. So maybe in this instance it was okay.

Or was she becoming a complete wuss woman? Was hot, down-and-dirty sex worth it? Yep!

Decision made, she quickly wiped her face, touched up her makeup, and put on a pair of flats. Not really sexy, but then again, neither was falling on your butt in front of an audience.

Glory actually smiled at Gabriel as she walked back into the living room; she spotted her panties where they still lay on the floor by the door and moved to get them.

"Leave them," he said firmly.

"I beg your pardon?" she asked incredulously.

"You gave up your right to wear panties when you argued with me, sweetness. Grab your purse and let's go," he said as he took her arm.

"You can't be serious," she said softly.

"Perfectly, are you ready or do you need a little more time over my knee before dinner?" His steely gaze pinned her as he waited for her to make the decision.

Glory nervously licked her lips and grabbed her bag, trying not to think about being completely bare under her skirt.

As they stepped out the door, a soft breeze blew up her skirt, making her nakedness impossible to ignore. What if a really strong gust came and did the whole Marilyn Monroe thing to her skirt? Everyone within eyesight would know her preferences regarding the style of her personal grooming. Would she spend every moment with this man blushing like a schoolgirl?

•••••••

Gabriel had a hard time not smiling in satisfaction as Glory followed his instructions with a minimal fuss. He knew it had been just a small skirmish and the battle was far from over, but it was best to start as he meant to go on.

She would always have rules he expected her to follow. In the end she would flourish under his guidance and care, but would probably have a sore bottom more often than not until she accepted her need for his dominance.

He enjoyed watching her struggle with her need to submit as it warred with her sense of what she thought she should feel about it. While feminism had its place, it had also caused a lot of problems for women like his Glory, who needed to submit in order to find the freedom to embrace who they were deep inside.

They'd get there.

Seating her in his car and buckling her in, Gabriel leaned in and placed a lingering kiss on her surprised mouth before closing the door and walking around to the driver's side.

"Where are we going?" she asked, obviously deciding to leave the small skirmish behind them.

"Maggiano's; is that okay with you?" he asked.

"Yes, I love their chicken parmesan," she said with a grin. He smiled with satisfaction as he put the car in gear.

Then Glory piled her purse and sweater on the console

between them and he frowned. He recognized the move for what it was; she was putting a physical barrier up between them. Gabriel's jaw tightened as he pulled over to the shoulder of the road.

Glory frowned over at him. "Why are we stopping?"

"I just figured out how you got to the ripe age of thirty-five with your virginity intact and thought we should discuss it," he said succinctly.

Her face filled with a riot of color as she gaped over at him. "I beg your pardon?"

"You're your own cock blocker," Gabriel informed her.

"What!" she screeched as her face got even redder.

"You put your purse and sweater up as a physical barrier between us, something men recognize around the world as a no-trespassing signal."

"I did not! I just needed some place to put my stuff and I…"

"No, you got nervous so you put them between us to defuse the sexual tension you felt," Gabriel said.

Glory gaped at him as her face continued to heat under his intense regard. She squeaked in alarm when he picked up her sweater and purse one at a time and tossed them in the backseat before leaning over the console and catching her shoulders firmly in his hands.

"One thing you need to understand about me, sweetness," Gabriel said as he pulled her inexorably toward him. "I will knock down every barrier—real or imagined—you try to place between us."

Then he took her mouth, stroking his tongue immediately inside to duel with hers until she whimpered and sagged against him as he devoured her, accepting nothing but complete surrender.

Gabriel gave her lower lip one last nibbling kiss, then gently sat her back in her seat, as she looked at him with wide dazed eyes.

"Are we understood?" he asked in a deep dark voice that brought forth another shudder in response to his words.

"Yes, sir," she said softly, slumping back in her seat with a sigh.

Gabriel nodded then pulled the car back onto the road, leaving Glory to ponder the fact that she didn't have complete control of the situation, and that the obstacles she was used to throwing in the way of suitors when she got uncomfortable wouldn't work with him. If she didn't want him to claim her and her virginity, she would have to actually force herself to tell him a firm no; otherwise she was fair game.

• • • • • • •

Glory expected dinner to be awkward at best after the little scene in the car, but surprisingly it wasn't. Gabriel put her at ease as soon as they sat down by regaling her with stories about his time on the Dallas police force.

Currently he was a sergeant with the SWAT team, but was weighing his options since he was close to his twenty years and was seriously considering leaving it to the younger guys on the force and taking retirement.

Glory totally understood. She told him about her own time as an investigator for CPS and how consumed she'd felt by the job and the horrible things she'd seen. It wasn't that she didn't care anymore when she left. It was just the opposite. She was filled with worry about the children she dealt with from the time she woke up until the time she went to bed, and at night she had nightmares about not being able to save them.

He took her hand when she told him she could remember every little face and everything they had told her about the atrocities that were visited upon them—things no adult should have to experience, much less a child.

Glory teared up. "So much innocence lost. You hope they'll be able to overcome what they've been through, but sometimes it seems so insurmountable. So, when my novels started selling well and it looked like I could make a living just writing, I handed in my resignation. It was a hard decision, but it was the right one for me. It was either that or go on antidepressants. It seemed much better to change my environment. I could never have become desensitized to hurting children and wouldn't want to be, but I feel like I did what I could for as long as I could and it was time to move on."

She smiled when Gabriel cupped her face in his hands and gently wiped the tears from her eyes with his thumbs. "No more tears. You made the right choice for you. I'm surprised you lasted as long as you did. Six years is a long time for CPS. The burnout rate is two-and-a-half years from what I've read."

"People come and go relatively quickly unless they're lifers. I really respect the ones that can stay, but I just couldn't do it anymore."

"So then you went on to write sexy books about spanking and BDSM," Gabriel said with a grin.

Glory gasped and looked around in case someone overheard. "Shhhh, you can't say stuff like that out loud!"

"I love how easily you blush," he said, leaning in close and nipping her lightly on the neck.

"Gabriel! We're in public!" she said, trying to scoot her chair away from his.

He stopped her by firmly grasping the back of her chair and tugging it until her chair scraped the floor, placing her tightly against him.

The loud noise of the chair going across the concrete floor made her cringe, but as soon as her body touched his, Glory couldn't help herself, sinking easily into his warmth. The man was positively addictive.

He took her mouth with another soul-drugging kiss that left her aching and hungry for more. She couldn't help but growl in frustration when once again he sat her back away from him and went back to eating like he hadn't just brought every girly bit she had wide awake and eager for action.

Glory glared at him from beneath her eyelashes before

spearing a piece of chicken with her fork.

His low chuckle of amusement further irritated her. "Did the chicken do something to you?"

She shoved her plate away from her in a fit of pique. "I'm done; can we leave now?" His hot and cold act was driving her nuts.

"Careful, little girl, you're cruising," he told her with an admonishing look.

Glory went from irritated to completely furious in an instant; coolly wiping her mouth on her linen napkin and dropping it on top of her plate, she stood up to glare down at Gabriel. "You know what? This is stupid and I'm done."

Grabbing her purse, Glory walked swiftly away from Gabriel and out the front door of the restaurant. She smiled thinly at the valet and asked him to call her a cab.

"That won't be necessary," Gabriel told him from behind her as she felt his hand close on her arm.

Glaring up at him in outrage, she tried in vain to tug her arm from his hold. "Let me go this instant!"

He tugged her up against him and leaned down to whisper in her ear, "I suggest you lose the attitude fast, young lady, or you'll feel the flat of my hand right here and now. Are you going to behave yourself or give this young man a free show?"

Glory felt her face heat up as she glanced nervously at the valet, who was watching them curiously. "I'm sorry; I won't need that cab after all."

"Good decision, sweetness," Gabriel said as he planted a hand in the small of her back and urged her into the parking lot. As he helped her into the car, Gabriel pulled her skirt up in back until her bare bottom was exposed.

"What are you doing?" she asked in alarm.

"I want your bare bottom sitting directly on the seat," he told her as he rolled the back of her skirt up until he could tuck the whole thing into her waistband.

Glory was scandalized; the front of her was completely covered, but anyone looking into the car would be able to see a large portion of bare hip on both sides where the skirt tucked behind her waist. "I can't ride all the way home like this!"

She moved around, achingly aware of the coolness of the leather seat beneath her and shocked by the escalating level of her own arousal. What was wrong with her?

Gabriel leaned in to loom over her seat, seeming to surround her with his body heat as he captured her eyes with his stern gaze. "You can and will ride home exactly like this with your bare bottom right there on that seat. I want to be able to look over and see that you're doing exactly as I instructed. Hopefully, by the time we get back to your house you'll be in the right frame of mind to apologize for your childish behavior."

Glory felt embarrassed tears begin to well up and she sniffed them back stubbornly. How had they gone from such a nice evening to this so fast?

He nodded at her, obviously satisfied for the moment she was going to obey him, and closed the door before walking around to get in on the driver's side.

As they made the drive back to her house, Glory began to cry as she thought more about their evening and the abrupt ending to dinner. She had behaved badly; his kisses had aroused her, which left her feeling achy and vulnerable, so she'd responded with temper because she hadn't known how to deal with it.

"I'm sorry, Gabriel," she said softly as he parked in front of her little house.

"I know you are, sweetness," he said tenderly, undoing her seatbelt and pulling her against his chest and dropping a kiss on the top of her head. "Are you ready for your spanking?"

Her shoulders slumped a little in acceptance as she took a deep breath, finding her senses filled with his scent. It seemed to wrap around her, making her feel safe and protected even though she knew he was about to burn her butt.

"Yes, sir," she said, releasing the breath she was holding with a shuddering gasp.

• • • • • • •

Gabriel nodded in satisfaction as he got out of the car and walked around to help Glory from her seat.

He stopped her when she would have pulled her skirt free of the waistband to cover her bottom. "Leave it."

"But we're outside. Someone will see me," she said, her eyes darting around nervously.

"I'll be behind you the whole way, Glory. No one will see, but you will leave your bottom exposed like the naughty girl about to receive a spanking that you are."

She looked up at him and obviously read the fact that he wouldn't bend on this issue in his face. She sighed and began the short walk to the house with her bare bottom on display.

True to his word, Gabriel stayed right behind her, making sure no one but he could see her exposed backside. He admired the milky white skin he planned to paint a hot shade of red as soon as they were inside. The color from the short spanking he'd given her earlier was already completely gone.

Gabriel planned on leaving a little more lasting reminder with her this time. The fight she'd picked in the restaurant had been just one more attempt to place a barrier between them. A barrier he would finish knocking down first by spanking her delightful bottom, and then second by giving her a little further punishment that would hopefully help her control herself a little better in the future.

Once they were inside with the door locked behind them, Gabriel led her to the couch and sat down with her standing nervously between his legs.

"Why are we here, Glory?" he asked in a tone that brooked no argument.

She flushed and looked down at the floor before softly answering, "I behaved badly at the restaurant."

"Yes, you did. You were very naughty. Why do you think that is?"

Glory shrugged and continued to stare at the floor.

"I asked you a question, young lady, and I expect an answer," Gabriel said sternly as he used one finger to tilt her face up to his own.

Her lower lip trembled as tears sprang to her eyes. "I don't know why I acted that way."

"I think you do, Glory. You were trying to drive a wedge between us again, weren't you?"

A lone tear trickled down her cheek as she nodded. "I'm sorry. You make me feel so out of control and nervous and I didn't know what to do, so I tried to push you away by behaving badly."

He smiled tenderly at her as he wiped the tear away. "What happens to naughty young ladies who misbehave?"

"They get spanked."

"How do they get spanked, sweetness?" he prompted her.

"They get spanked on their bare bottoms," Glory said, another telltale little shudder escaping her as she said the words.

"That's right. Naughty girls get spanked on their bare bottoms," Gabriel said as he pulled her down over one knee, catching her legs tightly between his own to ensure she was locked in place.

This time he wasn't playing at all; this was a no-nonsense punishment, so Gabriel began to slap his hand down hard and fast. Glory yelped and cried out as he methodically painted her backside an even shade of bright pink that blossomed down onto the tops of her thighs.

Then he lightly rested his hand on top of her quivering bottom. "Warm-up is done, sweetness. Now I am going to give you a lesson in proper behavior."

• • • • • • •

Warm-up? The actual punishment hadn't started? Glory wailed in response to his words, "Please! I won't do it again! I promise I'll be good!"

"I intend to ensure we don't have this particular discussion again, young lady. When I take you out on a date, you will ride home with me each and every time. You will not under any circumstances ever attempt to leave without me again. Am I understood?"

"Yes, sir!" she cried. Then she gasped in dismay when the arm around her waist tightened and he pulled her closer. The minute the hand resting lightly on her bottom left, Glory knew the brief respite was over.

His hand began to fall even harder and faster than before and she quickly realized the spankings she'd received before had been very mild. And she'd thought his hand was hard before… Again and again it fell with precision, so fast the number of spanks began to blur and she was only able to concentrate on the blistering heat filling her bottom.

"OOOhhhh! I'm sorrrreeeee!! Please!! I'm sorrreeeee!"

Then his hand started slapping down on her left sit spot, falling in the exact same place over and over until big tears were dripping down her cheeks as she begged him to stop. Mercifully he finally did, but then he started in on the other side.

Glory hollered and wailed her dismay as he moved on to the tops of her thighs. When the spanking finally stopped, there wasn't a place on her bottom or the back of her upper thighs that didn't feel swollen and scalded.

She just hung in place over his lap and cried as he gently rubbed her lower back in a soothing caress. Soon Glory found herself once again straddling his lap as she sobbed her apologies into his broad chest.

When she finally quieted, his soothing caress changed, his hand began stroking ever so lightly across the tender flesh of her bottom until it homed in between her thighs. Glory had a moment to be mortified at how wet she was before his finger sank deep and she no longer cared.

One finger quickly became two and soon she was riding herself closer and closer to an orgasm as she rose up and down to meet each thrust of his hand. Just as she was about to go over the edge, the fingers withdrew, making her groan in frustration.

"I think it's time I taught you how to please me, sweetness. Get on your knees," his dark voice instructed as he helped her to kneel between his spread thighs.

Glory licked her lips as she watched him slowly unbutton his slacks and lower the zipper to free a very long thick erection. He was bigger than she'd imagined, but the sight of his cock and the little bit of fluid leaking from the tip made her hungry in a way she'd never been before.

She'd read a lot of how to books on giving a blowjob and had practiced on her vibrator, a banana, and even a pretty big cucumber once, but she'd never actually had the chance to experiment on the real deal, so to speak.

It was shocking how much she wanted to taste him. Leaning in close, she nuzzled her face against Gabriel's groin, taking in his musky scent and licking lightly up his shaft until she was able to delicately lap at the fluid waiting for her at the tip.

As her tongue rolled lightly over the small opening, she was gratified to hear his hiss of pleasure and found the taste of him salty but faintly sweet. With a sigh of pleasure, Glory caught the base of his erection in her hand as she surrounded the plum-shaped head with her lips, sucking the tip of him in like her favorite lollipop.

Rolling him around in her mouth, she flattened her tongue against the underside of the head before releasing him from her mouth with a slurping pop.

Looking up at him, she stroked her hand up and down his shaft as she studied the heightened color of his cheeks. The thought that she was giving him such pleasure was a heady feeling and she was eager to take him deep in her throat.

With a sultry smile she leaned in and took his cock in her

mouth again, this time opening her throat as she took him as deeply as possible. She began a slow rhythm, taking him deep as she brought her hand up to meet her mouth, then stroking back down to his balls as she drew off of him, sucking hard the whole time, then licking at the head and paying special attention to the underside before sinking down on him again.

Gabriel was holding entirely still; she noticed his hands were locked down on the couch cushions at each side of him. Glory's heart swelled as she realized instead of taking command of the situation, he was giving her time to learn him and his body.

Remembering one of her manuals said swallowing would tighten her throat around the penis and increase the man's pleasure, Glory started swallowing when she'd taken him to the back of her throat. She did that two more times, managing to get more of him down each time before Gabriel took a firm hold of her head and held her in place.

"I'm going to cum now, Glory and I want you to swallow every drop like a good girl. Can you do that for me?" he asked.

She looked up, meeting his eyes, unable to answer verbally with her mouth stuffed so full, but she nodded and then swallowed around him again.

She reveled in the way his hands tightened in her hair as he began to thrust gently against the back of her throat as she continued to swallow every few seconds, then he stiffened and his shaft seemed to pulse in her mouth and throat just before he came, filling her with jet after jet of his creamy essence.

Glory swallowed everything he had to give greedily, finding she loved the taste as much as she was beginning to love the man. Then the thought of loving Gabriel was immediately dismissed; she wasn't ready to think about that yet.

She licked every trace of his orgasm from him before leaning back on her heels with a satisfied smile, then started when she realized he wasn't smiling.

"Where did you learn to do that so effectively?" he asked suspiciously.

Glory blinked. "Books, mostly, and I practiced. I wanted to be sure when the opportunity arose I was good at it."

• • • • • • •

Gabriel had been shocked by her apparent skill at cock sucking; it had actually been one of the best blowjobs he'd ever received, though part of his pleasure had been due to the obvious enjoyment she'd taken in the act.

He shook his head with a smile. Books, she said; only his little author. "What did you practice on?"

Glory blushed and looked at the floor again. "Mostly on my vibrator."

"You have a vibrator?" he asked.

She nodded, her face getting even redder.

"Bring it to me," Gabriel said firmly.

Glory got up off her knees and scampered to her room, her bright red bottom framed by the edges of her skirt where it was still tucked into her waistband. Gabriel took advantage of her momentary absence to tuck himself back into his pants and zip up.

She came back to stand in front of him, holding a purple jelly vibe with a funny-looking clit stimulator attached. It wasn't a rabbit, though the design was similar. He took it from her. "What's this one called?"

If Glory's face got any redder, he was afraid she'd burst into flame. "The eager beaver."

He barely managed to contain the laughter that threatened to burst from his throat; lord, this woman pleased him. Gabriel tugged her down to straddle his lap, facing away from him and moved his thighs apart spreading her wide.

Stroking his fingers into her wet heat, he smiled. "You're so wet, it's practically dripping down your thighs."

Glory made a strangled sound he was sure marked her embarrassment.

"You know you were a very bad girl, don't you, Glory?" he asked her as he continued to tease her slit with his fingers.

"Yes, sir," she whimpered as her hips bucked up toward his hand.

"Well, I'm afraid your punishment isn't quite over, young lady. I'm going to play with you for a little while, but you aren't allowed to come," he told her firmly.

"Okay," she said softly as she continued to ride his fingers.

Gabriel knew she didn't really understand that she wouldn't be allowed to come at all this evening, but she would soon enough. For his own sanity he decided to get the lesson over with quickly.

Removing his fingers from her tight heat, Gabriel took her vibrator, sent it all the way home with one hard thrust, and then turned on the little beaver.

Glory's back arched immediately and he had to wrap an arm around her waist to hold her in place. He began to thrust the toy in and out of her sheath in a hard fast rhythm, making sure the little vibrator caught her clit with every inward stroke.

"Ooohhh... oohhhh... yes... ohh... I'm going to come..." Glory panted, writhing with pleasure in his lap.

It took all of his resolve to pull the toy from her body just as she was about to come. He wanted to make her come over and over, but unfortunately that was for another day. Tonight he had a different lesson to teach; one that would be painful for both of them.

"Nooo... please! I was so close," Glory cried, then gaped at him in dismay when he lifted her from his lap and stood her between his legs once more. "Gabriel? I don't understand..."

"I told you, Glory, you aren't allowed to come. Not tonight. Bad girls don't get to come," Gabriel said resolutely.

"You can't be serious!" she exclaimed, obviously starting

to grasp the situation. "But you got me all worked up."

"I did. I needed to show you that your pleasure is at my discretion. You were naughty tonight and therefore as part of your punishment you aren't allowed to come. We will revisit the issue tomorrow if you're a good girl."

"You can't do this!" she wailed.

"Yes, young lady, I can and there will be no masturbating. If I find out you stole an orgasm from me, I will teach this lesson all night long, bringing you to the peak again and again with no relief. As a matter of fact, I'll be taking this with me when I leave so you won't be tempted to use it," Gabriel said, holding the eager beaver up to show her what he was talking about.

"That's my sex toy! It belongs to me, I bought it!" Glory yelled with a stomp of her bare foot.

"I agree this little silicon toy is yours," he said as he wrapped an arm around her waist and pulled her down on his lap again before boldly cupping her wet folds and sinking two fingers deep. "But this little eager beaver is mine and I will decide when it's pleasured, just as I will decide when it's punished."

He enjoyed the sight of Glory's head bent back over his arm, little mewling cries coming from between her pouty lips as he worked her almost to orgasm again and then flipped her face down over his lap just as she was about to come.

"No!!" she wailed, near tears in her frustration.

Gabriel brought his hand down on her already red bottom hard, delivering three swats to each cheek before lifting her to stand in front of him again.

"Are we understood?" he asked as he stood to look down at her.

"You're nothing but a… a… a big clit tease!" Glory gritted up at him before turning with her nose in the air and walking haughtily to her bedroom in a fit of high dudgeon. The effect was ruined when she bounced off the door facing, her still bare red bottom cheeks jiggling enticingly from the collision.

Glory sharply blew the hair out of her face as she glared over her shoulder at him. "Good night to you, sir!"

Her bedroom door slammed behind her, obviously dismissing him for the evening.

Gabriel couldn't contain the laughter coming from deep in his chest. Clit tease! She was absolutely adorable; he should be punishing her further for the little fit she'd just thrown, but his little author was new to D/s and she'd learned enough for one day.

He smiled as he grabbed his jacket and Glory's vibrator and let himself out after locking up.

CHAPTER SIX

Glory frowned as she shifted in her chair again on her tender bottom. Unlike after the last spanking, this morning she'd woken up with a definite reminder of her punishment in her nether regions.

She wasn't bruised, but her backside felt almost like it was sunburned, leaving it incredibly sensitive and tender.

The rest of her was achy from being horny. Glory was less sure how she felt about that particular punishment. On one hand she was so irritated with Gabriel for leaving her hanging like that she almost masturbated; but on the other hand she didn't want to risk missing out on what was sure to be a spectacular orgasm this evening to prove a point.

Her mama didn't raise an idiot after all!

The combined punishment left her so distracted though that she was finding it impossible to concentrate on her writing, so she decided to dedicate the day to research.

Glory was reading the ad section in the back of the *Dallas Observer* and almost choked on her hot tea.

There were coupons for a massage therapist with a picture showing her humongous boobs hanging out of her skimpy bikini top, but the ad that followed brought a blush to Glory's cheeks.

Let Me Soothe
Away Your Stress
Stress Relief with the Ultimate
Relaxation!
M–F 12pm–8pm

Wow! Glory knew there were ads like this in the back of smut magazines, but the *Dallas Observer?* Who'd have thought it?

She grinned to herself as she perused the rest of the ads.

Mistress Amanda
Beautiful Dominatrix
Sensual to corporal punishment

Briefly Glory wondered if Gabriel had an ad, then dismissed the thought. He didn't dominate for money; it was just who he was. These ads were greatness!

CANDI
Sexy college student
I need money for books!
What do I have to do to earn it?
Cause I will…

Seriously? Had these people heard of the Craig's List killer?

Single male wanting to meet
Females that are of the sunny
And assertive sort
Generous
Happy New Year!!
$75 early birds
$150 evening wakers
$250 night-timers

Incalls only from 7am–11pm

Glory blinked. Was this ad for a hooker? Was it legal in Texas? They could advertise?

Dallas Dolls
9 Girls
To choose from
$10 off with ad

Not only could they advertise, they had coupons!! This was too much to keep to herself. Glory shot a text to Nat.

I totally found an ad for a whorehouse in the Dallas Observer *and it has a coupon at the bottom of the ad for $10 off!*

A moment later, Glory's phone buzzed with Nat's reply.

What??? R U Serious? Hahaha!!!

Glory texted back, giggling at Nat's response.

Who would have thought hookers had coupons?

Not me!!! LOL!!

I wonder if they offer double and triple coupon days like the supermarket.

I don't know! Call and ask! Hahaha!!

Yep. Dallas Dolls, 9 Girls to Choose from

Oh my!!! U made me laugh for the day :))

I just had to share!

Thanks for sharing. TTYL. Love you!

Love you too!

Glory chuckled to herself. Too funny! Coupons! Unbelievable!

The doorbell rang as she moved on to some of the less entertaining ads, still sexual in nature but not nearly as fun. Still shaking her head, she swung the door open to find Gabriel standing on her front step.

He glared down at her. "Do you *ever* ask who it is before opening the door?"

Glory glared right back. "It's the middle of the afternoon!"

"Do you think all murders happen at midnight on foggy nights with a full moon?" he asked incredulously.

Glory heaved a longsuffering sigh. "Did you have a purpose for this visit or did you just come over to gripe?"

"I came over for a little afternoon delight, but I might need to take care of something else first," Gabriel said, raising a brow meaningfully.

She rolled her eyes and walked back inside, leaving him to follow her in and close the door. "Who said I'm in the mood for any delight?" With sudden inspiration, Glory scooped up the *Observer*, tore out the ad and coupon for Dallas Dolls, and handed it over to him. "Here ya go! Afternoon delight coming up and you even have a coupon!"

"Very funny; keep it up and I will delight in paddling your backside," he said with a grin.

Glory smiled back, walked slowly up to him, and circled her arms around his neck. "Hmmm, that doesn't sound all that delightful to me."

Gabriel cupped her bottom and lifted her against him. "I said I would delight in it, not that you would enjoy it," he said just before placing a few teasing kisses against her eager mouth. "Hi, sweetness."

"Hi, yourself," she whispered just before his mouth took

hers deeply, taking possession of her so thoroughly that she felt it to the tips of her toes.

She was so hungry for his mouth, she met his every demand with one of her own until they were both panting, needing much more than kisses, as pleasurable as they were.

Gabriel lifted her high in his arms and carried her to the bedroom, setting her lightly on her feet before catching the hem of her dress and skimming it over her head.

Glory stood in front of him in her bra and panties, feeling a little vulnerable with him still fully clothed, but seeing the hot need in his eyes as he looked his fill made her suddenly feel powerful.

He wanted her; she didn't understand why, but this smart, handsome, and dynamic man wanted her and Glory felt an answering need deep in her belly. Someday she might regret it, but for the moment she was his and he was hers.

"Strip," he instructed her succinctly.

Glory gulped, feeling her face go hot as she reached behind her and undid her bra before pulling it from her full breasts and dropping it on the floor in front of her. The smoldering look in his eyes as he drank in the sight of her unbound breasts boosted her courage. With her best imitation of a sultry smile and never breaking eye contact, Glory leaned over while hooking her fingers in the waistband of her sheer panties and pulled them slowly down her hips to below her knees where she let them fall around her ankles and stepped out of them.

Then tossing her shoulders back and standing proudly naked before him, she shot him a challenging look from beneath her lashes.

Gabriel smiled. "Beautiful." He sat down on the edge of her bed and pulled her to stand between his thighs.

"Move your legs apart, sweetness." He tapped lightly on her inner thighs until she straddled his right thigh. "Good girl."

She couldn't bite back a gasp when two of his fingers sank immediately into her wet heat.

"Look how wet you are for me, sweetness," he said, pulling his hand away from her to show her how slick and wet his fingers were before putting them back between her legs.

She groaned when his thumb slid inside rather than his fingers, the broad base of his hand pressing against her throbbing clit as the two fingers wet with her juices pressed insistently against her back passage.

"Relax and let me in," Gabriel commanded.

Glory shuddered and pressed against his seeking fingers with a deep breath and felt the stretch and burn as they penetrated her to the hilt. Then he started moving his hand, a very slight subtle movement, but it seemed to bring every nerve inside her roaring to life. The tip of his big thumb was riding against her g-spot in tandem with the fingers scissoring inside her anus as the base of his thumb seemed to vibrate against her clit.

"I... ohh... Gabriel!!" she cried out as she neared orgasm in what seemed like two seconds.

Gabriel used his other hand to bend her over until she had to press her hands to the mattress as she leaned over the leg she straddled and his other hand slapped down on her upturned bottom hard.

That one stinging swat was all it took to send her over the edge, but his hand continued to fall as she rode out her orgasm and went straight into a second one even stronger than the first.

Then her world shifted as Gabriel spun her around and laid her on the bed, still pumping his thumb and fingers inside her as he leaned in and took her throbbing clit between his lips and sucked hard.

Glory bucked up into him as she screamed his name. Then before her channel even stopped spasming, he hooked her knees over his arms and fitted the head of his cock to her and pressed inside to the hilt with one firm thrust.

Glory felt fuller than she'd imagined possible; none of her toys had prepared her for the reality of Gabriel's possession. She felt the stinging stretch of her body as it accepted a man inside for the first time, but the pleasure was indescribable.

He rested against her, not moving as her body became accustomed to him. Needing more, Glory began to wriggle as much as her position allowed. "Please... Gabriel... I need... more."

Gabriel withdrew slowly then drove back inside until she felt him butt up against her cervix. He continued stroking in and out of her in long, deep strokes until she was begging him to take her hard and fast.

Then he was slamming in and out of her with a force that shook the bed until she came undone around him, crying out and clinging desperately to his shoulders as she came through the storm.

"Good girl, I think we need to do that again," Gabriel said softly in her ear before pressing deep and rotating the head of his shaft against some magical spot inside that sent her into another orgasm that left her limp in his arms.

She could only groan when he began to move again, the sound of his body slapping wetly against hers and her keening cries filling the air. As the tension built again in her body to an unbearable level, those two fingers pressed back inside her tender asshole as he slid his other hand between their writhing bodies and began to rub her clit in a circular motion.

Glory's back bowed as everything inside her twisted and released in a climax that left her unable to even scream in its intensity, a gush of fluid bathing his cock as he stiffened above her, giving in to his own shattering climax.

In the aftermath, Glory's whole body shook as she began to cry. Gabriel rolled to his back, bringing her with him and holding her close.

"Shhhhh, my beautiful girl, I've got you... I've got you, baby," he crooned softly to her, cuddling her and pressing gentle kisses all over her face.

"I don't know why I'm crying," she sobbed into his

chest; she laughed when she realized she was crying on his still buttoned shirt. Curiously she raised her head and saw that his pants were bunched just below his ass.

For some reason the evidence of his own loss of control made her feel better. "You didn't get undressed."

Gabriel grinned sheepishly. "I couldn't wait any longer, sweetness. Next time we'll take the time to thoroughly enjoy each other's naked bodies."

She smiled up at him, running a finger lightly over his shirt. "I don't know, I think we enjoyed each other's bodies pretty good that time."

He smiled and placed a soft lingering kiss against her lips before getting up from the bed and hitching his pants up around his waist. "Be right back."

Glory watched from her position on the bed as he disappeared into the bathroom; she still felt too deliciously boneless to move. She heard the water running and figured he was cleaning up.

Grimacing at the sticky wet mess between her thighs, Glory knew she needed to make a discreet trip to the restroom herself. Then Gabriel was back a wet cloth in his hand; she frowned when he leaned down with an obvious attempt to clean her with it.

Immediately she began trying to scramble away from him, embarrassed by the thought of him cleaning her. "What are you doing?"

Gabriel stopped her retreat by catching her ankles and yanking her back down to the end of the bed. A sharp swat on the side of her thigh discouraged any further attempts to get away. "I'm taking care of you and unless you'd like a spanking, you'll be still."

She shuddered at his threat and felt a new flood of moisture between her legs as he bent and began to clean her with the damp cloth.

He spread her wide and even cleaned around her tender little bottom hole before taking the cloth back to the bathroom.

• • • • • • •

Gabriel returned to the bedroom and began stripping off his clothes as he studied his petulant-looking little author where she still rested on the bed. He folded them carefully so they wouldn't be wrinkled when he put them back on.

"Aftercare is part of it, sweetness; get used to it. I will always take care of you that way. To clean you up, but also to make sure you're okay and I wasn't too rough," he said softly as he lifted her up in his arms and pulled back the covers to tuck her into the bed before climbing in behind her and pulling her into his arms.

She relaxed into him with a sigh. "I suppose I can get used to it, but it was embarrassing."

He smiled and pressed a kiss into the top of her head. "Before long I'll know your body as well as I know my own and you'll know mine. There will be no room for embarrassment, unless of course you're being punished. That's an entirely different kettle of fish."

His lady love gave a very inelegant snort in response to that statement, which made him chuckle. Gabriel had a feeling she would always be a little bit of a brat. Something he would enjoy, but at the moment they had something serious to discuss. He'd forgotten to don a condom before sinking into her heat. A lapse he'd never experienced before.

"I didn't wear a condom," he said starkly.

Glory shifted in his arms and turned over in the bed to face him. She cupped his cheek in her hand and smiled up at him. "It's okay. I'm on the pill."

"It's really not okay, sweetness. I should have had this conversation with you before we had unprotected sex. I'm clean and haven't had sex without a condom since my wife died."

"Then there's nothing to worry about. We're both clean and I'm protected so we can dispense with worrying about condoms." Glory lifted her head and pressed a kiss to his chin before turning back over and snuggling back down.

Gabriel grinned. "Well, I'm glad that's settled." Then he lifted her leg to rest over his hip and slid inside her from behind.

Glory gasped as he filled her completely. He began to move slowly as he filled his hands with her breasts, plucking rhythmically at her nipples as he moved inside her.

He bit back a groan as her wet heat tightened around him with every twist of her nipples. "You feel so good around my cock, sweetness."

As one hand played alternately with her nipples, Gabriel's other hand skimmed down her stomach to play with her clit as his strokes got deeper and harder.

Glory raised her leg higher and pressed down to meet his hard thrusts, mewling little gasps escaping her with every breath.

He slammed into her hard, ground himself deeply inside her, and tweaked her little clit hard. "Come for me now, Glory."

She immediately tightened around him and came with a little scream as her hot channel began to milk him to his own release. As he came, Gabriel nipped her sharply on the spot connecting her neck and shoulder. She came again, and then went limp in his arms.

Gabriel lifted her leg back off his and spooned himself around her replete body, leaving them still intimately connected. She fell quickly asleep, her breathing settling in to a soft even rhythm. Gabriel snuggled in and closed his eyes, feeling completely at peace and like he'd finally found home.

They spent the afternoon napping and waking to make love again and again, breaking briefly for dinner, which was some frozen pizza Glory had in the freezer. Then they went back to bed to sate themselves on each other until they finally collapsed in each other's arms for the night.

CHAPTER SEVEN

Glory woke in mid-orgasm, Gabriel's face buried between her thighs. He looked up at her with a smile. "Mornin', Glory!"

She frowned, but before she could take him to task over his horrid use of her embarrassing name, he sank a finger into her ass as he sucked her clit hard.

Glory's back bowed and she came again as he continued to thrust his finger in and out of her eager back hole. Soon two fingers joined the first and three fingers were thrusting hard in and out of her tender orifice.

Gabriel brought her to three more screaming orgasms before pulling his fingers free and flipping her over. He pulled her up on her knees and slammed into her still pulsing sheath.

"One day soon, sweetness, I'm going to take this tight little ass," he told her, riding her hard and fast.

His words alone were almost enough to send her over the edge again; she pressed her chest down into the bed and spread her thighs even farther apart to take him as deeply as possible.

Gabriel slapped his hand down hard on her ass just as he made his final lunge, catapulting them both over the edge together. Glory couldn't believe she'd just woken up and already he'd left her feeling like a limp noodle.

With another slap to her bottom, Gabriel lifted her up over his shoulder and carried her into the bathroom with him. "Sorry to rush you, baby, but I've got to get to work," he explained as he set her on her feet in the shower under the warm spray. Gabriel made short work of soaping her body up, washing her tenderly between her legs and all around her sore anus.

He pushed her to stand directly beneath the spray to rinse off and wet her hair as he quickly scrubbed his own body.

When he began to work the shampoo into her hair, Glory quietly groused, "I could have done this myself, you know."

"I'm sure you could have, but I wanted to do it. I'm taking care of you, Glory. Do you really want to argue about it? I can spank you if you'd like, but I'd much rather pamper you a little this morning," he said firmly.

Glory decided to shut her mouth and just enjoy his tender ministrations. She had no desire to start the day with a real discipline spanking.

He rinsed the soap from her hair then worked in the conditioner. "Good decision, love."

She shut her eyes and pressed her head into his magical hands that massaged her scalp as he rinsed the conditioner from her hair. He was actually better than the shampoo girl at the salon. Of course she'd never made Glory come before washing her hair either.

All too soon it seemed their shower was over and he was rubbing her dry with one of her thick fluffy towels. Pulling her close, he kissed her deeply then set her away with a little pat to her bottom.

Glory followed him to the bedroom and watched him dress quickly in yesterday's clothes. He pressed another quick kiss to her mouth before heading out the door. "I have to go or I won't have time to stop at home for my uniform, but I'll see you tonight, okay? How about Chinese for dinner?"

"Sounds good," she said softly to his retreating back. Then he was gone.

Glory shivered as she enjoyed the unfamiliar twinges of soreness in her inner thighs and her more private areas. Gabriel had loved her so thoroughly that she knew she'd be reminded of him every time she sat down that day.

She smiled at the thought and moved to begin stripping her bed, knowing after the activities last night and again this morning, the sheets needed changing badly. The entire room smelled of sex. It was delicious.

Glory still had the same goofy smile on her face when her cell phone rang an hour later.

"Miss Glory?" the soft tearful voice asked hesitantly.

Glory frowned. "Julie?" Julie had been one of the kids she had on her caseload in foster care when she worked for the state. She'd had a horrible childhood and Glory had worked hard to earn her trust.

Glory was so proud when Julie graduated from high school; she'd grown far more attached to the girl than was advisable and had even given her private cell phone to the girl when she left foster care, telling her to call if she needed anything.

She hadn't heard from Julie in almost four years. Great heaving sobs came over the phone lines. "Julie? What's wrong?"

"Oh, Miss Glory, I'm in bad trouble. Linc's gonna make me have sex with his drug dealer friends on account he owes them money. I don't want to, Miss Glory, they're gonna hurt me. I told him I couldn't do it and he hit me and told me it wasn't up to me."

Glory felt something seize in her chest. Julie was such a sweet girl, she had to help her. Linc was another kid from her caseload. She'd tried to tell Julie he was trouble, but the girl always seemed to gravitate back to the little thug.

"Julie, where are you?" she asked as she grabbed some

of her old clothes out of the closet. She was no longer a caseworker, but she could look the part with a little effort.

"I'm in an abandoned apartment building on Washington Street in Dallas. It's a crack house now. It's dark…oh, Miss Glory, I'm so scared."

Glory was somewhat familiar with the area; there were a few old apartment buildings set for demolition mixed in with the new construction in the area. You went from good areas to bad areas within a block in that part of Dallas.

"Are you close to Fitzhugh, Julie?" she asked.

"I think so, about a block up on the left going toward Central," Julie said miserably.

"I'm on my way, honey," Glory reassured the girl.

"You're coming here?" Julie asked, sounding shocked.

"Well, no way am I leaving you there," Glory said firmly. "I'll be there in about twenty minutes, Julie."

"Hurry, Miss Glory, I don't know how long Linc will be gone," Julie said fearfully. "If he catches us sneaking out, it'll be bad."

"Hang on, honey," Glory said softly. "I need to go so I can get dressed and get there."

"Okay, bye," Julie whimpered and hung up the phone.

Glory dressed quickly in one of her old pantsuits and twisted her hair up in a no-nonsense bun.

As an afterthought she threw the little leather-encased bottle of pepper spray into her purse; it was best to be prepared. She was getting Julie out of that place come hell or high water.

As she drove, she dialed 911.

"Nine-one-one, what's your emergency?" the operator came across the line.

"My name is Glory Walters. A girl who was on my caseload when I worked for CPS called me. She's being held in a crack house on Washington Street against her will. I am on my way there now, but I'm afraid police intervention might be necessary."

"Ma'am, did you say you were on your way to the

scene?" the operator asked, sounding a little incredulous.

"Yes. She asked me for help."

Glory got on 75 and moved as quickly toward Fitzhugh as traffic would allow.

"It isn't safe for you to enter that scene. You could well create a hostage situation with two people being held instead of one."

"I know this isn't the best plan I've ever had, but I can't leave her there all alone. She was so scared. And she isn't going to blindly trust any officers she comes into contact with. I have to do this!" Glory said passionately. There was no way she was letting Julie face this situation alone. The girl had never really known what it was to be loved unconditionally and to have caring support. Julie had been scared and called her because she trusted her and no way was Glory going to let her down.

Glory left the line open, but ignored the rest of the operator's very reasonable arguments. Why respond when she knew this wasn't a situation in which she would be able to be reasoned with?

As she turned onto Washington Street from Fitzhugh, she watched closely for the abandoned apartment building. When she saw it, her stomach hit her knees. It was one long three-story building with every window boarded up. The big doors that had once graced the front of the building were long gone, seeming to open into a yawning darkness.

Glory drove past the place once, studying the area before turning around and finding a place to park across the street.

"I'm here. I'm not sure of the exact address but it's on the west side of the street on Washington between Fitzhugh and Ross. I'm sure the department is familiar with the place."

"Ms. Walters, I can't let you go in there," the woman said sternly.

"You can't stop me. I'm going to put my phone on speaker and slip you into my pocket so you know what's happening, but I am going in. Please don't talk anymore as it could cause more problems than help."

Glory put the phone on speaker then locked the screen before sliding it and the pepper spray into opposite pockets. She knew the police would send someone; she just hoped she got to Julie before they got there.

As plans went it wasn't great, but it was all she had.

Taking a deep breath, Glory climbed out and locked her car before crossing the street toward the big building. As she walked into the courtyard, she carefully stepped over several discarded needles, shuddering at the thought of accidently stepping on one and getting stuck.

Panic threatened to swamp her as Glory neared the open doorway and the darkness beyond it. Looking up, she saw a large bald black man leaning down over a balcony and watching her progression toward the door.

He had on sunglasses so she couldn't see his eyes, but she could feel them on her. Glory straightened her spine and lifted her head, staring straight ahead as she pretended to be unafraid.

What a joke! She was terrified. As Glory walked into the building, she turned left into a very narrow and dark corridor, the sound of frightened sobs coming from somewhere ahead; she hurried toward the sound.

Her eyes were adjusting to the darkness and she could make out a door on her right with a very small amount of light coming underneath it. The crying was coming from behind the closed door.

Glory knocked lightly and softly whispered, "Julie?"

The crying stopped and a soft voice spoke from directly behind the door. "Miss Glory?"

The door quickly opened and a small figure hurled itself into Glory's arms. She caught the girl's trembling form and held her close as she blinked at the sudden light from inside the room. It wasn't very bright coming in from where someone had chipped a hole in the wood covering one of the windows, but it was welcome in the face of such inky darkness.

"We've got to get out of here, Julie," Glory said quietly. "If we hurry, maybe we can…"

The press of something hard in the small of her back stopped her words short. "Who'd you call, Julie? I told you we don't have a choice. If you don't give it up, they'll kill me."

Glory and Julie were shoved back into the room. Glory spun around to face the man with the gun and backed away from him, pulling Julie with her. She recognized Linc almost immediately.

His dirty blond hair was sticking up in several directions, his face scarred and pockmarked from the years of drug use. Suddenly he smiled, revealing blackened teeth, "Miss Walters? Really, Julie? This is who you called? What do you think she can do? Now I have two women to give them. It'll definitely put me in good with 'em, might even give me some free product."

"Linc, this is a really bad idea. You'll go to prison for the rest of your life if you don't stop this right now!" Glory said sternly as she pushed Julie behind her; the frightened girl clutched her shoulders nervously.

"Shut up, lady! You ain't got say-so over me anymore! In fact, the way I see it now I have say-so over you! Maybe I'll have you suck my dick before I hand you over to the guys. I bet you're real good at it."

Linc moved toward her, already starting to unbuckle his belt, reaching out to touch her face with the end of his gun.

Glory moved almost without thinking. Bringing her fist up on the inside of the wrist holding the gun, she slapped the back of his hand as hard as she could simultaneously with the other. Surprisingly, it worked and the gun flew out of his hand across the room.

Before Linc could recover from the shock, Glory stepped forward and jammed her foot into the front of his knee as hard as she could, hearing a cracking sound as Linc crumpled to the floor holding his knee. Glory kicked him in the groin as soon as he was down for good measure, grabbed the gun, and backed up to a wall with Julie, pointing the gun at the injured man crying on the floor.

Her hands were shaking, but she knew she could shoot if she had to.

"Where'd you learn to do that, Miss Glory?" Julie whispered in her ear, her thin body still pressed tightly against Glory.

"When I worked for DADS, they had a guy come in and give us a quick self-defense class. That move is all I remembered; actually, I'm kind of surprised it worked," Glory said with a shudder.

As the minutes wore on she found herself getting more and more shaky. Suddenly she remembered the phone in her pocket and scrambled to get it. "Hello?" she asked, hoping the operator was still there.

The operator gave an audible sigh of relief. "Is everyone okay, Ms. Walters?"

"Yes, but I'm hoping help is on the way?" She voiced the statement as a question.

"The SWAT team is already on site, ma'am, just stay put and they will come to you," the operator instructed.

A knot formed in the pit of her stomach. "Did you say SWAT team?" Glory had a feeling Gabriel would be less than pleased about her little adventure.

· · · · · · ·

Gabriel sat in the front of a squad car resting his head on the steering wheel. He'd bowed out of the raid. He was too emotionally involved with the situation since his girlfriend was in the building surrounded by gang members. He would put the rest of his team at risk if he went in with them.

Usually cool under fire, Gabriel was surprised to find himself almost shaking at the thought of Glory in there surrounded by God knows what. He'd already watched his wife die an agonizingly slow death; the thought of losing

Glory too almost unmanned him.

Gabriel could hear what was going on with the raid in his earpiece and was relieved when he heard Ramirez enter the room where Glory was and ask her to put down the gun.

"You're not gonna believe this, sarge, but your girl disarmed the suspect and has been holding him at gunpoint with his own gun," Ramirez said into his ear and Gabriel could hear the smile in his voice.

While Gabriel was relieved she was safe and had been able to protect herself, he was a long way from smiling. Now that the danger and fear had passed, he'd skated past relief and straight into outrage that she'd put herself in harm's way.

When she and a small thin blond girl were walked out toward the waiting ambulance to be checked by the EMTs, Glory looked up and spotted him. At first she smiled and started toward him, but then she stopped and stood still, biting her lower lip nervously, watching his face as he approached.

Gabriel grabbed her to him, hugging her hard before setting her away and giving her a little shake. "What were you thinking? You could have been killed! Confronting a man with a gun? Even coming to a place like this at all was…"

"But Gabriel…" she began.

He held his hand up. "No, I won't listen to any excuses from you. There aren't any acceptable excuses for this."

"I had to, Gabriel… I…"

"No. I can't do this right now. I can't deal with you. Ramirez?" Gabriel handed Glory off to the other man and walked away. He was so angry with his little author. If she'd uttered one more word of her excuse, he wouldn't have been able to stop himself from jerking her over his knee, pulling down those sensible pants, and paddling the daylights out of her in front of his entire team and the ambulance guys.

Not a good move for a guy two months away from

retirement. And probably not a good move for his relationship with Glory. You didn't punish when you didn't have control of yourself and he was way too angry to lay a hand on her.

As he walked away, intent on joining in the search for drugs and illegal weapons, Gabriel looked over at her once where she now stood with an EMT.

Glory looked over at him and he could see the way her chin wobbled that she was close to tears, but Gabriel steeled himself against the pitiful slump of her shoulders. It would do her good to stew in her own juices a little.

Focusing on work would do a lot to help him clear his head. Shaking his head, he joined his men.

CHAPTER EIGHT

Glory couldn't believe it had ended like that. She sat staring morosely at her computer screen, unable to write anything.

Gabriel hadn't listened to anything she'd tried to say, he'd just said he couldn't deal with her and walked away.

She'd understood from the beginning that she could hardly expect anything permanent from a man like Gabriel. After all, he had his choice of all the beautiful submissives at his club; why settle on a chubby, middle-aged author?

Glory sighed. Permanent, no, but she'd still thought he cared more about her than to just walk away without a word. It had been two days and she hadn't heard anything from him.

To her the sex had been earth-shattering, but she supposed it wasn't very realistic to think it had been anything out of the ordinary for him. In fact, he was probably already boffing his next conquest.

She tried to tell herself it didn't matter; sure, it was great sex, but now she knew what she was looking for and she'd find great sex again. Glory ruthlessly tamped down the little voice in her head that said she'd never find another man like Gabriel. No one else would be able to make her body sing like he had.

At least she'd gotten to talk to Julie yesterday at the DA's office. In exchange for Julie's testimony against Linc and the gangbangers he was staying with, the DA had arranged for Julie to go to a really good rehab program out of state. By the time the trial rolled around, Julie would be clean and ready to start her new life.

Glory teared up again as she remembered the conversation with Julie as they prepared to say goodbye for a few months.

Julie had suddenly looked up at her and softly whispered, "I wish you were my mother."

Glory had been beyond touched and she'd hugged the girl close. "Thank you, Julie, but you need to give your mom some credit. If I'd had a baby at fourteen, I might have made some of the same mistakes she did."

Julie had hugged her back and said fiercely, "No, you wouldn't have."

Glory stepped back and cupped Julie's face in her hands. "I hope I wouldn't have, but we'll never really know. What I do know is that I love you and I will support you and do everything I can to help you make a future for yourself. I want you to spend your time in rehab really thinking about who you want to be, who you deserve to be, and what you need to do to accomplish that. You deserve a good life, Julie, and I know growing up in foster care was beyond hard, but you can get past it. You can take advantage of the fact that when you age out of the foster care system in Texas, they'll pay for your education anywhere in the state. Don't let the opportunity pass you by."

"Yes, ma'am," Julie said softly. "I won't let you down, Miss Glory."

Glory grinned. "You won't ever let me down, honey. I just don't want you to let yourself down. I may get on your nerves every now and then because when people care, they don't always keep their opinions about what you should and shouldn't do to themselves. I know I certainly won't."

Julie grinned tearfully. "I'm glad."

It had been really hard for Glory to finally say goodbye and leave the scared little girl inside a twenty-one-year-old's body behind. She sat still, lost in her musings about Julie and then again about Gabriel.

Glory shook herself to clear her head and then stood up with determination. Now that she and Gabriel were no longer an item, the club was no longer off limits. She could carry on with her research.

• • • • • • •

A few hours later she was standing in the club next to the bar, nursing the one drink she was allowed. She'd donned the outfit she'd worn the first night, the purple bustier and short black skirt with the four-inch heels she barely managed to totter around on without busting her ass.

"You sure it's okay with Gabriel that you're here?" Marcus, one of the other owners of the club who was tending bar, asked.

"I told you he no longer cares what I do, Master Marcus. I'm a free agent again," Glory said, wincing a little at the twinge of bitterness she heard in her voice.

"Good God, it's that idiot Perry," Marcus said with a frown. "I can't deal with him tonight. Seems like a good time to get something from the back."

Glory smiled as Marcus made a hasty exit from the bar area and sent one of the club's employed submissives to mind the bar.

"Look what we have here. A little fat slut for my enjoyment," a high-pitched nasal voice said from directly behind her. "What's your name, girl?"

Glory started when a hand clapped lightly off her bottom and turned to glare at the man behind her. "Well, it certainly isn't girl, nor do I appreciate the moniker fat slut."

He was short with thinning hair and an obviously puffed-up sense of importance. "Watch your tone with me,

74

young lady. I have little patience for sass."

Glory rolled her eyes and turned back to the bar. "No, thank you."

"I beg your pardon? Did I tell you to turn around? Look at me when I'm speaking to you, young lady," the creepy little man said sharply as he grabbed her arm and spun her back to face him.

"Let go of me, you creep! I already said no, thank you. I'm not interested in playing with you," she said, jerking her arm from his grasp.

Red began to creep up the little worm's neck as he glared at her. "You will speak to me respectfully, or I will get a gag!"

Glory sighed. "Look, I'm sorry we got off on the wrong foot but don't scenes need to be negotiated?"

"Well, yes," the man admitted.

"Well, there you go. I'm not interested in negotiating a scene with you. I'm sorry if you felt I was disrespectful, buddy, but respect is a two-way street. Now, my name is Glory Walters and I'm an author here to do some research for my next book," she said, hoping to defuse the situation.

"An author, well, then you need some experience to write about in your little story. I would be happy to give you some. You can use me as a character. My name is Dom Perry Yoane."

Glory blinked as the man looked at her proudly. "You're kidding, right?"

He frowned. "Kidding about what?"

"You can't seriously expect me to believe that's your name. It's ridiculous! Hey, you might make a good character for my book though," Glory said conversationally.

The man perked up, momentarily forgetting she'd called his name ridiculous. "Really?"

"Yes, of course, every book needs at least one pretentious ass in it," Glory said matter-of-factly.

Dom Perry's face turned completely purple in his rage. "You little bitch!"

Glory was a little startled when he raised his fist and started to swing and breathed a sigh of relief when Gabriel suddenly appeared, caught his fist, and then handed him off to Marcus.

"Perry, what have I told you about harassing submissives? You're done here. The fact that you would ever raise your fist to a woman says you're abusive," Marcus told him before dragging the complaining man away.

Glory grinned, enjoying watching the odious little man get his just deserts. Then a firm hand clamped down on the back of her neck, pulling her up on her toes.

"I do believe I told you the club was off limits." Gabriel's stern voice sent shivers down her spine.

Glory looked up at him as he turned her to face him. "But you broke up with me so I thought…"

"No. I told you I couldn't deal with you right then. Trust me, sweetness, you should be glad I stepped back. If I'd reacted as I wanted to in that moment, every member of my SWAT team would have seen me turn your bare bottom an impressive shade of purple and you might never have sat again," he told her succinctly.

Glory barely had time to register his words before he looked down at her feet. "I also said you were no longer allowed to wear heels. How many rules have you broken recently, young lady?"

"I… ummm…" Glory faltered, more than a little nervous about the look in Gabriel's eyes.

"Step out of your shoes," Gabriel instructed.

"What?"

"Step out of your shoes. You don't want to make me repeat myself again," Gabriel said firmly.

Glory gulped and stepped out of her shoes. Gabriel held his hand out and pointed to them wordlessly. With a sigh she leaned down and picked them up in order to hand them to him.

"Missy!" Gabriel barked and suddenly a very pretty blonde completely naked except for her bunny ears was beside him.

"Yes, sir?" the girl asked, her head bowed respectfully.

"You've been a good girl lately. What size shoe do you wear?" Gabriel asked her, never taking his eyes of Glory's.

Glory stood still in shock as she realized his intent.

"Seven, sir."

"I believe these are the perfect size then," Gabriel said before handing the girl Glory's shoes.

"Thank you, sir!" Missy said with a grin before dancing off with Glory's heels in hand.

"You can't give away my shoes!" she exclaimed.

"I just did," was his only response.

"But those were four-hundred-dollar shoes! They're worth more than that, I got them on sale at T.J. Maxx!" Glory cried as she watched her shoes rapidly disappearing with the gorgeous blonde.

"Glory, I'll buy you a hundred pairs to replace them; they just won't have heels. Stop worrying about the shoes, little girl. You have much bigger things to worry about right now."

Glory gasped when, taking a firm hold of her arm, Gabriel marched her over to a low bench and sat down before dragging her face down over his lap. He pulled her skirt and panties completely off, leaving her bare from the waist down.

"Wait… can't we discuss this? It was just a simple misunder… *owwww!*" Glory yelled as the palm of his hand landed hard on her left bottom cheek. Her worries about being so exposed in a room full of people quickly fled under the rapid onslaught of his heavy hand.

"Owwww… please, Gabriel…" she cried as her bottom filled with stinging heat.

"Please who?" he asked cracking his hand down even harder.

"*Sir!* Please, sir!" she yelled.

"You will address me appropriately when you're being disciplined," Gabriel instructed as he continued to impart the error of her ways to her upturned backside. "I'm very unhappy that once again you put yourself in harm's way."

"But he was touching me and not taking no for an answer!" Glory tried to defend herself.

"That's why safewords and dungeon monitors are in place. If you'd asked, someone would have intervened immediately. However, if you'd followed the rules I put in place for your safety, this situation would never have arisen."

Stopping the spanking for a moment, Gabriel tipped her further over his knee and slid a finger into her dripping heat.

Glory groaned, mortified by her arousal from such a stern spanking. A public spanking at that! Then she yelped in alarm when he withdrew his finger after coating it thoroughly in her juices and spread her bottom cheeks to sink it deep into her tender little pucker.

"Naughty girls get their bottoms punished inside and out," he told her as he began thrusting his finger in and out of her backside in a punishing rhythm. "Missy!"

"Please... noooo... oh, please..." Glory cried out and squirmed over his knee as he continued to discipline her bottom hole. The eager blonde suddenly popping back up next to them as if nothing out of the ordinary was happening completed her humiliation.

"Yes, sir?" the girl said, obviously only too happy to do his bidding.

"I need you to get a few things from my office. I'll need a small butt plug, the Cracker Barrel paddle, as well as the board of education." Gabriel gave the list of items quickly, each one sounding more horrible than the last to Glory.

"I'll be good! I promise! I'll never do it again, sir!" she begged.

"Sweetness, I can guarantee you'll never do it again," Gabriel assured her.

• • • • • • •

Gabriel continued to work his finger in and out of her tight hole, enjoying the sight of it disappearing inside her, framed by her reddened bottom cheeks.

Glory had finally submitted completely to her punishment, collapsing over his lap and emitting the occasional grunt as he punished her little rosebud.

He had barely been able to believe his eyes when he'd spotted her in the club being accosted by that idiot Perry. Wannabes like Perry were a large part of the reason he didn't want her in the club until he felt she was ready and better able to handle their advances.

There were a lot of gray areas in the BDSM world that required careful negotiation to ensure everyone's freedom to explore while also making sure they were safe.

Missy returned and happily handed him a small purple butt plug. Gabriel couldn't help but grin. He wondered if Glory would appreciate the fact that Missy had obviously tried to match the plug to her bustier.

"Missy, could you squeeze a little lube on this for me?" Gabriel felt Glory cringe over his knee, having Missy help him even a little with her punishment adding to her embarrassment.

Missy helpfully squeezed the lube on the plug for him and watched as he removed his finger from Glory's helpless bottom and began to work the little plug inside. It was a small plug, but still thicker than his finger had been.

Glory arched her back and moaned as he began to work it in and out of her until he finally seated it fully inside.

Missy handed him a wet wipe for his hands then stepped away at a jerk of Gabriel's head. The paddles had both been laid helpfully under Glory's nose so she could look at them while he got the butt plug inserted.

"Glory, hand me the small paddle, please," Gabriel instructed firmly.

With a shuddering sigh, she reached down and picked up the small Cracker Barrel paddle and then handed it to him, looking up at him with pleading eyes as he took it from her.

"Face front," he said implacably. With a defeated slump of her shoulders, she fell back into place over his knees.

Gabriel trapped her legs between his own to help her keep position. "Now you will receive a paddling for coming to this club without permission and once again wearing heels."

"Yes, sir," she said meekly.

He raised the paddle then brought it down crisply on the left side of her bottom. Glory's reaction was immediately; she jerked and cried out at the intense sting left in the wake of the little paddle.

Gabriel wasted no time in bringing the paddle down again and again all over her cringing backside. He left no part of her bottom untouched and didn't stop until her entire backside was a brilliant shade of scarlet from the middle of her crack to the top part of her thighs.

He paused, resting the paddle lightly on her bottom. "Now, do you think you have a better understanding of my expectations, young lady?"

She was barely able to sob out her answer. "Yes, sir."

"What are my expectations?" he asked.

"I'm... n-never to come to the club without your express permission. I'm not to be rude and I'm not to wear heels." The words were stilted and difficult to understand through her sobs, but she got them all out.

"Very good. Now I'm going to finish your spanking with six more swats and then you're going to bend over this bench with your bottom on display for thirty minutes and think about why you were punished. Do you understand?" he asked sternly.

"Yes, sir," she whispered through her tears.

Gabriel nodded and then tilted her hips even further over his knee. The last six swats would be delivered directly to her sit spots. The hand on her lower back moved to pull the skin of her bottom up a little to ensure each and every swat had the maximum effect.

He delivered the hardest swats yet—three in the exact same place on each side of her bottom that brought a keening wail from his little author.

Holding her in place, Gabriel rubbed her back a little until she calmed, then helped her into place over the bench. While he didn't enjoy delivering harsh punishments, Gabriel did enjoy the site of her well-punished bottom on display with the base of the purple plug winking out from between her cheeks.

Standing, Gabriel held up the long thick school-type paddle. "If any dom or domme catches my sub in this club without me, please deliver ten swats with the board of education and then stand her in a corner to await further discipline from me."

• • • • • • •

Glory cringed at his words and the answering cries of agreement from throughout the room. Her bottom was throbbing inside and out, as she knew was Gabriel's intent. She was beyond embarrassed to imagine the sight she must make with her big red bottom on display complete with butt plug.

Then Gabriel knelt in front of her and placed the big long school paddle in her outstretched hands. "You will hold this while you contemplate your punishment. Your thirty minutes starts now."

She held the heavy paddle and knew without a shadow of a doubt she never wanted to feel its sting. The small wooden paddle Gabriel had just wielded so thoroughly was all he needed to get his point across.

Glory sniffled miserably. Her bottom was on fire and she was sure her face was just as red; she was so embarrassed to be in this position showing her naughty bottom to all and sundry. Gabriel was quite serious about his rules.

It occurred to her that as thorough as the punishment had been, Gabriel had never once mentioned her adventures at the crack house. Her bottom flinched as she wondered if that meant she still had more punishment coming.

As sore as her bottom already was, Glory couldn't imagine taking further punishment on it. She'd never sit again!

Suddenly she felt warmth at her back as Gabriel's big hand grasped her once again by the nape of her neck as he leaned over her. "Are you thinking about what you could have done differently?"

"Yes, sir. I'm sorry I came to the club. I really thought when you told me you couldn't deal with me that you were done." Glory felt tears gather in her eyes once more as she remembered how hurt she'd been.

"Shhh, I love you, Glory. I'm still not very happy with you and we have a lot to discuss once we're back at your house. You took your punishment very well; will you be able to take the rest of what you've earned as gracefully?" Gabriel asked.

She shivered as his breath fanned her sensitive ear. Glory wanted desperately to please him, but the thought of more spanking scared her even while his dominance sent another wave of heat to pulse between her thighs.

His broad palm stroked across her tender bottom lightly, as if enjoying the heat radiating off of it.

"You've been a very naughty girl, haven't you, Glory?" he asked her as his hand skimmed down her bottom, tapped the end of the plug seated so deeply inside her, and then his fingers sank into her waiting heat. "You're all wet, sweetness. Such a needy girl you are, is this for me?"

"Yes, sir… only for you…" Glory panted as he began to slide the plug in and out of her bottom again while the fingers of his other hand drove in and out of her quivering sheath and his thumb strummed over her clit in a circular motion.

Gabriel worked her expertly to the edge before stopping and soothing her with wide sweeping strokes down her back. Once she was calm, he went right back to using his fingers and the plug to drive her right back to the edge.

Glory clung to the paddle in her hands like her life depended on it as her need grew and grew until she was whimpering and pleading for release.

"Do naughty girls get to come?" Gabriel asked.

Glory started to cry. "No, sir. Naughty girls don't get to come. Only good girls get to come. I'm so sorry!"

"I know you are, sweetness. I'm not ever going to have to repeat this lesson again, am I?" he asked her.

"No, sir," Glory wailed. She felt so lost; adrift on a sea of pain and need, she ached. She wanted nothing more than for Gabriel to drop his pants and sink his cock into her depths. Wanted it so badly, she didn't even care about the public setting anymore, but she knew he wouldn't. Not tonight.

Gabriel bent down and took the paddle from her before helping her to stand. When he dropped the paddle and opened his arms, Glory flew into them, desperate for the shelter they provided.

He scooped her up in his arms and carried her to an oversized chair, sitting down with her in his lap. She snuggled into his chest and cried quietly against him while he stroked her hair and pressed comforting kisses to the top of her head.

Someone dropped a blanket over her; Gabriel immediately cocooned her in the blanket before tilting her a little away from him and holding a cool bottle to her lips. "Drink this, baby, you need it."

Glory obediently opened her mouth and began to drink greedily as soon as the cool water hit her mouth, suddenly realizing how thirsty she was. She finished the entire bottle with him holding it for her. "Thank you," she said softly before pressing her face back to his chest.

"Did you get enough?" he asked.

"Yes, sir. I'm ready to go home," she said quietly from her place against his shirt.

"All right." Gabriel lifted her to her feet then, picked up the blanket and her skirt, and folded them over one arm as he guided her toward the front door.

"Ummm, I need my skirt," Glory whispered up at him as she tried to stop their forward momentum. She was horribly conscious of being completely bare from the waist down and somehow just being in the bustier made her feel even more exposed.

"You'll walk to the car as you are," he told her firmly and continued to propel her toward the door.

"I'm practically naked!" she exclaimed, chewing worriedly on her lower lip.

"The club is secluded; you won't be seen by anyone but other members. I need you to show me that you can obey me," Gabriel said succinctly.

Glory took a deep breath; this was a test. She'd already failed the obedience test rather spectacularly today and she wanted to please him, so she walked in front of him without further complaint. She knew instinctively now was not the time to bring up the plug still riding high in her ass either.

She blushed profusely when they stopped at the front desk to get her purse and Gabriel chatted to the guard like escorting a half-naked woman outside was an everyday occurrence. Glory had to give props to the guard; he didn't even seem to notice her or her state of dress.

She watched silently as Gabriel fished her car keys out of her purse and handed them to the guard. The guard said he would arrange for it to be dropped off at her house.

Gabriel escorted her to his car and helped her to slide into the front passenger seat. Glory hissed as her punished bottom came in contact with the seat and then again when sitting pushed the plug in deeper.

"Show me you can ride home without complaining and I'll take the plug out when we get to your house," he told her with a gentle smile.

"Yes, sir," Glory said as he buckled her seatbelt and then closed the door.

"I'm proud of how well you're taking your punishment, Glory," Gabriel told her after getting in on the driver's side. He picked her hand up and placed a soft kiss on her palm.

The ride to her house was quiet; neither of them seemed to feel much like talking. Glory knew there was still a reckoning due about the choices she made in her efforts to save Julie. She just really hoped it wouldn't be tonight. Her head hurt from crying and her bottom was really sore.

After he pulled into her driveway and cut the motor, Gabriel handed her the blanket. "Wrap this around yourself to get into the house."

Glory wrapped the blanket around her waist as he walked around to open her door. Gabriel helped her from the car, her purse and skirt under one arm.

He already had her keys in his hand so he quickly opened the front door and urged her inside.

"Drop the blanket," he said as soon as the door closed behind them.

Glory immediately obeyed.

"Good girl. Now I want you to go and bend over the arm of the couch," Gabriel instructed.

Suppressing a sliver of worry, Glory did as he asked and bent herself over the arm of the couch.

He was right behind her and stroked a hand over the punished flesh of her bottom; nudging her legs apart with one foot, he gently pulled the plug free from her.

Glory groaned as the plug slid free of her aching hole. She was amazed at how bereft she felt now that it was empty.

"Stay here," he instructed as he left the room; she could hear water running in the bathroom. He must have been washing the plug.

She gasped when she felt a warm wet cloth cleaning the tender area; a little embarrassed, but Glory knew better than to kick up a fuss about aftercare.

Gabriel patted her lightly on the bottom. "Good girl. Now I want you to go change into your nightgown and then

85

come back. We need to have a little talk before I go."

She shot up from her position and turned to face him in alarm. "You're leaving?"

"We'll discuss it in a minute. Mind me, please."

"Yes, sir." Her shoulders slumped as she walked to her room.

• • • • • • •

Gabriel watched his little author walk slowly from the room, the dejected slump of her shoulders making him want to gather her close and assure her everything would be okay.

He just wasn't sure it was. They needed to have a very frank discussion on what each of them expected from a relationship before things went any further. Gabriel needed to know she would accept his guidance and discipline. If she couldn't do that, as much as it would hurt, their relationship was already dead in the water.

Gabriel sat down on the couch as Glory walked hesitantly back into the living room. The uncertainty on her face struck him low in the chest.

He opened his arms to her. "Come here, sweetness."

Glory came quickly to him and sat on his lap, wincing slightly as her sore bottom came in contact with his thighs. Gabriel cuddled her close and kissed the top of her head.

"First, I want you to know I'm completely and totally in love with you, Morning Glory Walters…" Gabriel began.

Glory's head sprang up, tears filling her eyes, "Oh, Gabriel, I…"

"Let me finish," he admonished gently before continuing. "I love you, but you need to understand this is who I am. I like to scene at the club and role-play, but when it comes to domestic discipline, I'm not playing. I will be the head of my household; there are rules that I will expect to be followed and consequences if they aren't. I will always listen to your opinions and value everything you have to say. In many areas of our lives together there will be room for compromise, but you need to understand domestic discipline won't ever be one of them. I will give you a fair hearing, but if I decide punishment is warranted, you will be punished."

"I know," she said softly, looking down at where her hands rested in her lap.

He tipped her face up to his with his finger forcing her to meet his gaze. "Do you really, Glory? Tonight was the first serious punishment you've ever received from me. You need to really think about how you felt about it because there will be times I will leave your bottom sore inside and out if what you did merits a severe punishment. Tonight was the tip of the iceberg."

She shivered in response to his words and tears spilled down her cheeks as she looked up at him. "But I love you."

He smiled sadly at her. "I know you do, sweetness, but you need to decide if you love me enough to completely submit and trust me to guide you and take care of you the way I think is best. Even when that entails discipline you might not agree with at the time. I will never punish you in anger, but that doesn't mean you won't have a hard time sitting sometimes."

Glory nodded as he cupped her face in his hands, using his thumbs to wipe away her tears. "You still have a punishment coming if you choose to pursue a relationship with me. It will be severe. I'm still having nightmares about you in that place with those gangbangers. I'll plug you again, paddle you with that Cracker Barrel paddle until you're howling, and I'll take a strap to you. Then when you're a very sorry little girl, you'll take my cock in your ass."

Glory's eyes widened as she began to stammer nervously, "Oh... I... I don't know, Gabriel... I..."

"You don't have to make a decision right now. In fact, I don't want you to. I want you to think about everything I've said and about what you want and need. If you decide to commit to me and submit, you'll need to ask me for your punishment and tell me why you deserve it."

A flush filled her cheeks as he lifted her from his lap and stood. Gabriel tilted her face up to his and took one sweet kiss from her trembling lips. "I love you, sweetness, but the ball is in your court. I hope to hear from you soon."

Setting her away from him, Gabriel walked out the door without looking back. It was the hardest thing he'd ever done.

As he closed the door, he heard Glory dissolve into broken-hearted sobs. He steeled himself against going back inside and left.

· · · · · · ·

Glory didn't think she'd ever stop crying after Gabriel left. She really loved him, but could she completely submit to him?

Her bottom hurt so badly after the paddling he'd given her; it was difficult to imagine a strapping on top of it. As it was she was fairly certain she'd be feeling tonight's spanking for at least a day or two.

When she'd looked in the mirror while she was putting on her nightgown, her bottom was still a bright cherry red and a little swollen. Glory sighed, knowing that while her bottom was incredibly tender, he hadn't really hurt her or done lasting damage.

She also knew she would think about the rules she'd broken every time she sat and think twice about breaking them again. Wasn't that the purpose of discipline?

Fresh tears gathered in her eyes as she considered a life without Gabriel in it. He was right; she had a lot to think about.

CHAPTER NINE

It was a week after the night Gabriel had spanked her and Glory still hadn't made her decision. She didn't know if she was more afraid of life with Gabriel or life without him. In all fairness, her fear of life with him wasn't so much of Gabriel or the punishments she was sure to earn, but more of her reaction to them.

Glory knew a part of her, hidden deep inside, both craved and needed his discipline and that scared her more than anything. What kind of person did that make her? She was a vibrant, independent woman able to take care of herself. Why then did she have this need?

Most of her struggle in making the decision rested on her fear of herself. The part of her that got wet and aroused from even his most severe spanking. Not because of the pain, but his control and dominance over her. Shouldn't her need and lack of control be something she was ashamed of? How could she possibly embrace it?

A little hanky-spanky in play was one thing, but this was a lifestyle she was considering.

A couple of days after the spanking, a package had arrived with two pairs of very expensive slave sandals. They were of course flats, but still sexy and feminine. They made her smile wistfully as she recognized this was another way in which he was caring for her; he told her she couldn't wear heels, but was supplying something just as beautiful and flattering so she would still feel sexy without them.

Gabriel was a wonderfully loving and caring man; she just had to trust herself enough to take him up on what he was offering.

• • • • • • •

It was Saturday night and eight days since her talk with Gabriel. Nat and Jessica were over for a girls' night of pizza and beer and she was explaining her dilemma to them.

"I just don't know what to do," she said softly as she took another sip of beer.

"Let me get this straight, you love him. He wants to spank you and have you call him daddy while he gives you mind-blowing orgasms…" Jess said matter-of-factly.

Glory sputtered as she choked on her beer. "He never asked me to call him daddy!"

Jess waved a hand at her, unconcerned with her outrage. "Whatever, it's just semantics; it all has a deliciously paternalistic feel."

Glory frowned at Jess, unsure how to respond to her remarks.

"Let's not lose track. The important thing is Gabriel loves you and you love him. Yes?" Nat asked.

"Yes. I really do love him," Glory told her earnestly.

"Then why would this decision be so difficult?" Nat asked with a little heat. "Do you think the real deal comes along every day?"

"No joke," Jess said with feeling. "Are any of us with the love of our lives? You have the chance to be, so quit dicking around."

Nat rolled her eyes. "Nice, Jess."

Jessica shrugged. "I call 'em like I see 'em."

"Glory, let's be honest. You aren't running from Gabriel

here, you're running from yourself. The thing is, honey, you're never going to get away from you," Nat said, then hugged her close when Glory teared up. "I know this is scary, but if you don't grab this opportunity with both hands, you'll regret if for the rest of your life."

"I know," Glory said miserably.

"Oh, for God's sake! You like having your ass smacked. What's the big deal here? Lots of women and men do. It's how you're wired." Jess drove straight to the heart of the matter with her usual sensitivity.

Glory blushed and sucked the rest of her beer down in one big gulp before reaching for another bottle. "Am I really that obvious?"

"Glory, you write spanking and BDSM erotica, of course you're bent that way!" Jessica said baldly.

"Exactly," Nat said. "You've found the perfect guy, who is into all the things you are and probably ready to teach you a few more. You love him and he loves you. So tell me again why you're sitting here drinking beer with us?"

Glory sat up straighter. "You're right! I love him and don't want to live without him."

"Go get him, girl!" Nat and Jess cheered in unison.

She looked at her friends a little nervously. "He's going to spank me so hard. I'm still in trouble for getting Julie out of that crack house."

"In that case, have him give you a couple of good ones for me," Nat said with a frown. "I still can't believe you did that, what would we have done if... something had happened to you, Glory?"

Guilt hit her low in the gut when Nat got choked up on her last words. She hadn't thought about how her actions affected anyone but Julie at the time. She'd scared all of her friends and her family. Gabriel was right to want to give her a severe punishment.

She just needed to step up and take what she had coming. Downing another beer for Dutch courage, Glory picked up her phone and called Simone.

• • • • • • •

Gabriel sat morosely in the lounge area of the club nursing a scotch, Marcus and Simone sat bickering quietly near him. It was a typical Saturday night at the club. The background was full of the sounds of flesh meeting flesh or other things and the smell of sex.

It had been a week and two days since he'd seen Glory. He'd even sent her shoes and received not a peep from her in return. She wasn't going to choose him. He'd gambled and lost.

Gabriel was no longer sure it was a gamble he should have taken; he needed her like the air he breathed. Maybe he could live without the domestic discipline. It went against everything he believed in, but the thought of living without his little author made him doubt himself.

He frowned as he heard a drunken little giggle and looked around and nearly dropped his scotch. A very naked Glory was crawling toward him, sporting a tiny pair of rounded ears on top of her head and what looked like beaver teeth in her widely grinning mouth. If he wasn't mistaken, a broad paddle-like tail rested against her bare bottom.

"What on earth are you doing?" he exclaimed.

Finally reaching him, Glory rose up on her knees unsteadily, placed a hand over his crotch with a drunken leer, and said, "Your little eager beaver would like to swallow your pole whole."

Next to him, Marcus choked on his beer and Simone pounded him helpfully on the back.

"You're drunk!" Gabriel exclaimed incredulously.

Glory gave him a wide beaver toothy grin. "I shoved a beaver tail butt plug up my ass and crawled in here naked to tell you I love you and accept any discipline you think I need. You think I could do that sober?" She finished by closing one eye and looking him up and down to assess his reaction.

"How did you get in here drunk? It's against the rules!"

"Simone helped me!" she said with a grin.

Gabriel shook his head and shot a dark look at the domme before lifting Glory to her feet and bending at the waist to toss her over one broad shoulder.

"Heeey! I'm upside down! Oooh, I love your butt!" she exclaimed as she reached down with both hands to cup the aforementioned area.

Praying for patience, Gabriel braced her with one hand on her bottom directly beneath the paddle-like beaver tail and headed toward the elevator that would take them up to his apartment over the club.

The loud slap of a hand hitting a bare bottom rent the air, followed by an agonized yelp.

He felt Glory brace her hands on his back to straighten up enough to look toward the sound. "Wait! That man is spanking Simone!"

"Good!" Gabriel said succinctly. "It's about time."

"But I want to see…" she said petulantly.

Gabriel snorted; so much for female solidarity. Apparently when drunk, Glory really embraced her voyeuristic side. "You worry about your own backside, young lady. Believe you me, it's all you can deal with right now."

"Oh, yeah," she said softly as she slumped down again against his back.

He couldn't help but grin as he patted her bottom. "Oh, yeah, is right."

By the time they made it inside his apartment and he'd bent her over the sink in the bathroom to remove her beaver tail, Gabriel's little author was close to falling asleep.

"I appreciate the sentiment, my eager little beaver, but from now on nothing goes in your ass or anywhere else that I don't put there or instruct you to. Understand?" he asked.

She pressed her face into her arms and lifted her bottom for him to remove the tail. "Yes, sir."

After carefully removing the tail and then cleaning up both it and Glory, Gabriel lifted her high in his arms and carried her to bed.

"You aren't gonna spank me?" she asked with a yawn.

"Not tonight," he said as he gently tucked her under the covers. Then he stripped before climbing in on the other side and pulling her into his arms.

Glory snuggled in close. "Love you."

Gabriel kissed the top of her head, at peace for the first time in over a week. "I love you too, sweetness."

CHAPTER TEN

Glory awoke to a pounding in her head and pressure in her bladder. She lay still for a minute as she tried to decide if the pain in her bladder was worth moving and jostling her poor head further.

Her bladder finally won out and she headed groggily to the bathroom; spying the abandoned beaver tail in the sink, she felt her face fill with heat. She couldn't believe she'd done that! After the beers at her house and a couple of shots with Simone up in her apartment, the idea had seemed brilliant. Now it seemed silly and she was beyond embarrassed.

Gabriel probably decided she was way too big a nut to tie himself to permanently, she thought as she took care of business and washed her hands.

"Good morning, sleepyhead," Gabriel said, leaning against the bathroom door with his arms folded watching her.

Glory blushed and looked at the floor. "Are you going to punish me now?"

"Not right this minute," he told her.

"Don't worry, you're still getting that pretty bottom punished, but first I think some eggs, Advil, and coffee are in order," he added as he took her by the arm and led her into the kitchen.

"Can I at least have a shirt," she asked, feeling very vulnerable being completely naked with him dressed.

"Nope," he said as he seated her at the table.

Glory frowned as she sat down in front of a plate of scrambled eggs and toast. "I'm not sure I can eat…"

"Too bad. Your body needs it and you'll feel better faster if you do. Eat your breakfast." His tone left no room for argument.

She tentatively took a bite of eggs and hoped it stayed down. When it did, she took another bite and soon realized he'd been right; the food was settling her stomach. When she'd finished her plate, he placed two Advil on the table in front of her with a big glass of water.

Glory gratefully accepted both and with Gabriel's encouragement drained the glass of water after swallowing the pills. Her reward was a hot cup of coffee.

They sat quietly talking about nothing as she finished her coffee. By the time she'd finished her second cup, Glory realized she felt almost back to normal.

"Feeling better?" he asked.

Glory smiled. "Yes. Much, thank you."

"Good. Now I want you to go take a shower and then stand in the corner by the closet when you're finished. I expect to find you completely naked with your nose in the corner, thinking about why you're about to be punished," Gabriel instructed her.

She felt her mouth dry out as she looked at him.

"Now, Glory." The words were spoken quietly, but the command was implicit and she found herself springing to her feet and hurrying from the room.

Glory showered quickly, washing away the last vestiges of her little drinking binge the night before and contemplated the punishment to come. This was going to be bad.

• • • • • • •

Gabriel found her exactly where he'd told her to be, naked with her nose in the corner by the closet. As he watched, every few seconds her bottom clenched as if anticipating the coming spanking.

With a smile he turned and got the things he needed from the locked wardrobe in his bedroom. He laid them neatly out on the bed for his use and moved the trashcan next to the bed before calling her over to him.

Glory turned and walked toward him, pausing momentarily when she caught sight of the strap, paddle, and medium-sized plug lying on the bed.

He held his hand out and gestured for her to come the rest of the way; she took a deep breath and walked up to take his hand.

"Good girl," Gabriel praised her before pulling her to lie across his thighs. He would start with a hand spanking to warm her up. It would help to prevent bruising, although with the intense punishment she had coming, a little would still be possible.

Glory squealed when the first slap of his hand landed on her left butt cheek. He simply pulled her in closer as he began to pepper her bottom with hard fast swats, bringing it quickly up to a hot pink hue as she kicked her legs in response.

"That's enough of that, young lady," he said sharply as he delivered three hard smacks to each sit spot. "This is just your warm-up and you are carrying on like I've already lit your tail on fire."

She whimpered, "I'm sorry, sir. I'm just worried about how bad it's going to be."

"Well, if you don't settle down, it will be considerably worse," Gabriel informed her. "Why are you here over my knee, Glory? Why are you getting your bare bottom spanked so soundly today?"

"Because I put my safety at risk by going into that crack

house to help Julie," she said quietly.

"What should you have done?" he asked.

Glory took a deep breath. "I should have let the police handle it."

"Was that suggested to you?"

"Yes, sir. The 911 operator told me not to go in, that help was on the way, and I went in anyway," she said miserably.

"The first part of your spanking is going to deal with that; during your strapping we'll discuss the issue of confronting an armed gunman," Gabriel told her. Then he handed her the Cracker Barrel paddle she remembered so well. "You'll hold this while I insert your butt plug and think about what you could have done differently."

Glory took the paddle. "Yes, sir."

Gabriel picked up the plug and the little bottle of ginger oil lube. Coating the plug liberally, he tilted her further over his knee and spread her bottom cheeks open with one hand before gently working the tip of the plug into her tight little rosebud.

"Ooooh… Gabriel!" she cried, even as she spread her legs apart to make it a little easier for both of them.

"This is what happens to naughty little girls who put their lives in danger. They get their bottoms punished inside and out," he told her resolutely as he began to work the plug in and out of her bottom, getting it in a little deeper with each movement.

Glory groaned as he finally worked it deep inside. Her muscles loosened to let it in and then tightened back up around the base. He pushed on it with the end of his finger and got another soft groan in response.

Soon the heat from the ginger oil would begin to make itself known. His little author would remember this punishment for some time to come.

"Hand me the paddle, Glory, and ask for your spanking," Gabriel instructed.

She gave an embarrassed little moan before handing him

the paddle and looking up at him over her shoulder. "Please give me the spanking I deserve for putting myself at risk, sir."

"Very good," he said, giving her back a little rub before taking the paddle in his right hand and lifting it high.

The first crack of the paddle left her gasping and struggling to climb off his lap, but Gabriel held her fast and delivered another stroke almost immediately. He quickly paddled her, alternating from cheek to cheek until they were both a hot cherry red. From there he moved to the tops of her thighs and worked down and back up over her entire bottom.

Glory began to wail. "It hurts, ooooh, my bottom burns! What is that?"

"Ginger oil lube I used on the plug; it will help you not to clench and also help you to focus on your bottom," he explained. "Now I'm going to finish your paddling, and then you'll go back to the corner for fifteen minutes before we take care of your strapping."

Then he tipped her further over one leg and clamped her legs between his own; these last twelve swats would all be on her sit spots.

He crisply delivered the hardest six swats yet to the tender crease where her bottom met her thigh on the left side.

"No... stop... not in the same place! Spank somewhere else! Please!" she yelled.

Always happy to oblige, Gabriel delivered the last six to the exact same place on the other side. By the time he was finished, Glory was sobbing quietly over his knee. He rubbed her back for a minute and let her settle down before helping her up and leading her to the corner.

• • • • • • •

Glory sniffled quietly in the corner, resisting the urge to rub her bottom. She knew that wouldn't be well received, but it was burning inside and out. The thought of the strap falling on her well-paddled backside was anything but pleasant.

All too soon her fifteen minutes were over and Gabriel called her back to him. She moved quickly, not wanting to earn anything extra.

"Bend over and place your hands flat on the end of the bed," he instructed.

As soon as she was in position, he tapped her thighs to widen her legs and then she felt him rubbing something slick into her clit. She was embarrassed by the wetness she knew was leaking down her thighs.

The embarrassment was quickly chased away by the building heat in her clit; he'd put the same stuff burning inside her bottom on her clit!

"Ohh… ohhh… please, Gabriel! It burns!" she cried as she began shifting her hips around.

A firm slap to the back of one tender thigh made her freeze in position. "Breath through it, eventually the burning will start to feel good," he told her as she felt him catch hold of the plug buried deep in her ass and begin to rock it in and out of her.

She shuddered, pain and pleasure seeming to intertwine as he worked it in and out of her tender bottom. The heat inside her and building on her throbbing clit seemed to somehow morph together until she was actually thrusting her bottom up to meet each thrust of the plug. Just as she thought she might come, he seated the plug fully inside her once more.

"Good girl. Now we'll take care of your strapping. Why are we here?" Gabriel asked.

Glory swallowed. "I confronted an armed man and took his gun."

"It was blind luck that you were able to get the gun away from him instead of being seriously hurt or killed," he told her matter-of-factly.

"I know, sir. I'm sorry. I promise I'll never do it again,"

Glory said tearfully, her remorse evident.

"I intend to make sure you don't," he told her firmly. "I'm going to give you twelve strokes. Can you tell me what's going to happen after your strapping is finished?"

"Then I'm going to take your cock in my ass," she said, a shiver running through her as she told him. Glory was dreading it, but also looking forward to the experience.

"That's right, because bad girls take it up the ass," Gabriel said.

Glory felt his hand come to rest in the small of her back, petting her softly before he picked up the strap. She heard it whistle through the air before it impacted her tender posterior.

She stiffened as a line of fire filled her bottom directly over her sit spots; the stroke also jolted the plug in her bottom, sending it even deeper and reawakening the burn inside.

Gabriel wasted no time; the next stroke fell before she could even completely register the first and then the rest quickly followed until she had her face pressed to the mattress sobbing out her apologies.

She heard the strap hit the floor and then Gabriel spread her legs even farther apart as he pulled the plug from her. She heard a crinkle of a foil packet as he unwrapped a condom and then he was there, the broad head of his cock pressing against her for entrance.

Glory moaned and found herself pushing back against him and bearing down to help him inside.

The burn of her clit and her anus seemed to intensify as he began to work himself in and out of her. He took her slowly and carefully, allowing her body to stretch to accommodate his girth and length.

One hand worked itself between her thighs and began to insistently rub her swollen and throbbing clit. Glory pushed back harder against him in response, suddenly wanting all of him.

"Please, Gabriel... oh, please..." she panted.

Then finally he was all the way inside; she felt full and completely owned by him as his balls pressed up against her. Then he started to move; he pounded her hard and fast, his pelvis slapping against her punished bottom as his fingers worked her greedy little clit.

Glory came almost immediately, but still he continued to work himself in and out of her at a furious pace. Then he pinched her clit as he slammed home one last time and ground himself inside her as he released.

She felt his cock jerk deep inside as she came again, her bottom tightening around his spasming cock. Glory collapsed face first onto the bed unable to move, completely wrung out from her punishment and the intense orgasms he'd just brought from her.

Gabriel withdrew gently from her bottom, and she whimpered slightly as he pulled from her tender hole.

"Shhh… stay right where you are, sweetness," Gabriel told her as he left the room. Then he was back with a wet cloth. He cleaned her thoroughly, the coolness of the cloth a relief to her burning bottom.

Glory heard him moving around, taking care of things like the plug and putting up his implements, she supposed. She faintly heard running water.

Then he was back, scooping her up against him as he carried her to the bathroom. She gasped as he lowered her into a hot bath, wincing as it first came into contact with her punished flesh.

"It'll feel better in a minute, sweetness," Gabriel assured her, kneeling at the edge of the tub to tenderly wash her and massage her body beneath the water until she was the consistency of a limp noodle. "You took your punishment so well. I'm proud of you."

Glory smiled sleepily at his words. "Thank you for taking care of me."

"I'll always take care of you, sweetness. I love you and want to spend the rest of my life with you," he told her as he let the water out and gathered her up in a big fluffy towel.

"Really?" she asked softly. She knew what he'd told her, but a part of her had been afraid to believe it was true.

"Really. I plan to have Glory in the morning for the rest of my life, sweetness," Gabriel told her as he picked her back up and carried her to bed.

"I love you, Gabriel," she told him as she wrapped her arms around his neck.

"I love you too, sweetness, and I plan to spend the rest of the day in bed showing you how much."

He laid her on her back in the middle of the bed and came down over her body; Glory opened her thighs wide to welcome him home. They both groaned as he sank into her heat.

Gabriel's hands reached under her to cup her sore bottom and tilt her hips for deeper penetration as he began to take her hard.

"Look at me, Glory," he demanded.

Glory looked up, her breath catching in her throat as she met the intensity of his gaze. Never breaking eye contact, he took her up one peak after another, barely letting one orgasm end before the next one started.

"Who do you belong to, Glory?" he asked her as he bottomed out against her cervix.

"You... only you..." she cried.

"Now and forever," he said as he stiffened above her.

She reveled in the feel of his seed filling her as it splashed hotly against her inner walls, triggering another orgasm of her own.

He collapsed against her, his face resting in the curve of her neck. Glory ran her fingers through his hair as she held him close. "Now and forever."

EPILOGUE

Happy to be home, Glory smiled as they pulled up in her driveway. They'd just dropped Julie off in San Angelo. She would be starting school there in a few weeks and had agreed to live with a friend of Gabriel's off campus.

She'd been living with them for the last few months and Gabriel obviously cared just as much about her as Glory did.

They'd discussed the risks of relapsing back onto drugs and how important structure was for her, especially right now. Julie had admitted that a structured environment would work best for her and had agreed to moving in with Luke and following his rules. Luke would take care of her and make sure she had help with her school work when needed.

At first, Glory had been a little nervous about Julie moving in with a dom, but Gabriel had reassured her that he'd known Luke for years and everything would be all right. Luke wasn't looking for a playmate, but he would be able to give Julie the structure she needed.

They'd all agreed Julie needed to be away from Dallas and all of the people she'd hung around with there. It would be too easy for her to fall into old habits if she stayed in the area for school.

As hard as it was to leave Julie in San Angelo, Glory knew it was for the best and they'd have her home on holidays.

The last six months had been wonderful. She and Gabriel had gotten married in a small ceremony with friends and family in attendance. Gabriel and her father got on like a house on fire, and her mother adored him.

Glory also finished her BDSM novel and based it largely on her relationship with Gabriel. It was a bestseller.

The only thing that seemed off about the last few months was Simone. Glory hadn't seen her friend since the night she'd dressed like a beaver and Marcus had spanked her. Marcus wasn't talking, and Gabriel had told her to mind her own business.

Since she'd learned it was best for her bottom to listen to her husband on such matters, the mystery of Simone was something that would keep until Simone was ready to explain things.

Gabriel smiled at her as he pulled up in front of their house. "I was thinking steak sounded good for dinner. What do you think?"

"I think that sounds perfect!" Glory said with a smile, but then frowned. "I don't think we have any in the freezer."

"It wouldn't thaw in time for dinner anyway. I'll run to the store while you work on the sides," he told her.

Glory agreed and climbed out of the car after giving him a quick kiss. Walking into the house, she stopped in front of the large picture of Michelle in the hallway.

Before they were married, Gabriel had told Glory all about Michelle and his first marriage. When they'd moved in, she'd insisted on placing Michelle's picture on the wall in their home with the rest of the family photos.

Glory winked conspiratorially at the blonde woman's smiling visage and ran a gentle hand over the soft swell of her belly as she thought about the secret she planned to share with Gabriel later.

As she walked into the kitchen, she couldn't help but feel Michelle was smiling down on them with approval from above.

THE END

Made in the USA
Middletown, DE
23 October 2020

22643511R00064